ALBERT CAMUS

Exile and the Kingdom

ALBERT CAMUS was born in Algeria in 1913. He spent the early years of his life in North Africa, where he became a journalist, and from 1935 to 1938 he ran the Théâtre de l'Équipe, a company that produced plays by Malraux, Gide, Synge, Dostoyevsky, and others. During World War II he was one of the leading writers of the French Resistance and editor of *Combat*, an underground newspaper he helped found. His fiction, including *The Stranger*, *The Plague*, *The Fall*, and *Exile and the Kingdom*; his philosophical essays, *The Myth of Sisyphus* and *The Rebel*; and his plays have assured his preeminent position in modern letters. In 1957, Camus was awarded the Nobel Prize for Literature. Upon his untimely death in a road accident in 1960, Jean-Paul Sartre wrote, "Camus could never cease to be one of the principal forces in our cultural domain, nor to represent, in his own way, the history of France and this century."

ORHAN PAMUK is the author of a memoir, *Istanbul*, and five novels, including *Snow* and *My Name Is Red*, which won the 2003 IMPAC Dublin Literary Award. His work has been translated into more than forty languages. In 2006 he was awarded the Nobel Prize in Literature.

CAROL COSMAN has translated works by Jean-Paul Sartre, Honoré de Balzac, Simone de Beauvoir, and many other writers from the French.

VINTAGE

INTERNATIONAL

Exile and the Kingdom

ALBERT CAMUS

Exile and the Kingdom

STORIES

TRANSLATED AND WITH AN INTRODUCTION
BY *Carol Cosman*

FOREWORD BY *Orhan Pamuk*

Vintage International

VINTAGE BOOKS   A DIVISION OF RANDOM HOUSE, INC.   NEW YORK

FIRST VINTAGE INTERNATIONAL EDITION, FEBRUARY 2007

Translation and Introduction copyright © 2006 by Carol Cosman
Translation of Foreword copyright © 2007 by Maureen Freely

Library of Congress Cataloging-in-Publication Data
Camus, Albert, 1913–1960.
[Exil et le royaume. English]
Exile and the kingdom : stories / by Albert Camus ;
translated and with an introduction by Carol Cosman ;
foreword by Orhan Pamuk.—1st Vintage International ed.
p.   cm.
ISBN 978-0-307-27858-6
I. Cosman, Carol. II. Title.
PQ2605.A3734E913 2007
843'.914—dc22
2006037914

Book design by Steve Walker

www.vintagebooks.com

Printed in the United States of America
10   9   8   7   6   5

CONTENTS

FOREWORD *by Orhan Pamuk*

We admire writers first for their books. But as time goes on, we cannot remember reading them without also revisiting the world as we then knew it and recalling the inchoate longings that they awoke in us. We are attached to a writer not just because he ushered us into a world that continues to haunt us, but because he has made us who we are. Camus, like Dostoyevsky, like Borges, is for me one of those elemental writers. Their metaphysical prose ushers the reader into a mysterious landscape that we long to understand; to see it take on meaning is to know that literature has—like life—limitless possibilities. If you read these authors when you're young, and in a reasonably hopeful frame of mind, you will want to write books as well.

I read Camus some time before I read Dostoyevsky and Borges, at the age of eighteen, under the influence of my father, a construction engineer. In the 1950s, when Gallimard was publishing one Camus book after another, my father would arrange for them to be sent to Istanbul, if he was not in Paris to buy the books himself. Having read them with great care, he enjoyed discussing them. Though he tried from time to time to describe the "philosophy of the absurd" in words I could understand, it was not until much later that I came to understand why it spoke to him: this philosophy came to us not from the great cities of the West, or the interiors of their dramatic architectural monuments and houses, but from a marginalized, part modern, part Muslim, part Mediterranean world like ours. The landscape in which Camus sets *The Stranger*, *The Plague*, and many stories in this volume is the landscape of his own childhood, and his loving, minute descriptions of sunny streets and gardens that belong neither to the East nor to the West made it easy for us to identify with his work. There was also Camus the literary legend: my father was as enthralled by his early fame as he was shaken by the news that he had died, still young and handsome, in a traffic accident the newspapers were only too happy to call "absurd."

My father, like everyone, found an "aura of youth" in Camus's prose. I sense it still, though the phrase now reflects more than the age and outlook of the author. When I revisit his work now, it seems to me as if the Europe in Camus's books was still a young place where anything could happen. It is as if its cultures had not yet fissured; as if you could contemplate the material world and almost see its essence. This may reflect the optimism of the postwar period, as a victorious France reasserted its central role in world culture, and most particularly in literature. For intellectuals from other parts of the world, postwar France was an impossible ideal, not just for its literature, but for its history. Today we can see more clearly that it was France's cultural preeminence that gave existentialism and the philosophy of the absurd such a prestigious place in the literary culture of the 1950s, not just in Europe but also in America and non-Western countries.

It was this kind of youthful optimism that prompted Camus to consider the thoughtless murder of an Arab by the French hero of *The Stranger* a philosophical rather than a colonial problem. So when a brilliant writer with a degree in philosophy speaks of an angry missionary, or an artist grappling with fame, or a lame man mounting a bicycle, or a man going to the beach with his lover, he can spiral off into a brilliant and suggestive rumination on matters metaphysical. In all these stories, he reorders life's mundane details like an alchemist, transforming its base metals into fine philosophical prose. Underlying it there is, of course, the long history of the French philosophical novel to which Camus, like Diderot and Houellebecq, belongs. Camus's singularity is his effortless melding of this tradition, which relies on an acerbic wit and a slightly pedantic, somewhat authoritarian authorial voice, with Hemingwayesque short sentences and realistic narration. Though this collection belongs to the tradition of the philosophical short story with Poe's and Borges's work, the stories owe their color, vitality, and atmosphere to Camus the descriptive novelist.

The reader is inevitably struck by two things: the distance between Camus and his subject, and his soft, almost whispering mode of narration. It is as if he seems unable to decide if he should bring the reader deeper into the story. The reader is left hanging between the author's philosophical worries and the text's descriptive demands. This may be a reflection of the draining, damning problems that Camus encountered in the last years of his life. Some find expression in the opening paragraphs of "The Voiceless" when Camus alludes, somewhat self-consciously, to the problems of aging. In another story, "Jonas, or The Artist at Work," we can sense that Camus at the end of his life was living too intensely and that the burden of fame was too great. But the thing that truly damned and destroyed Camus was without a doubt the Algerian War. As an Algerian Frenchman, Camus was crushed between his love for this Mediterranean world and his attachment to France. Whereas he understood the reasons for the anticolonial anger and the violent rebellion it had unleashed, he could not take a hard stance against the French state as Sartre did, because his French Algerian friends were being killed by the bombs of Arabs (or "terrorists" as the French press called them), fighting for independence. And so he chose to say nothing at all. In a touching and compassionate essay he wrote after his old friend's death, Sartre explored the troubled depths concealed by Camus's dignified silence.

Caught between French colonialism and the love of his French Algerian friends and pressed to take sides, Camus chose instead to explore his psychological hell in "The Guest." This perfect political story portrays politics not as something we have eagerly chosen for ourselves, but as an unhappy accident that we are obliged to accept. It is difficult to disagree . . .

Translated by Maureen Freely

INTRODUCTION

This volume of Camus's short stories, most of them written between 1949 and 1955, has been for half a century a literary treasure hidden in plain sight. Although the first English translation of *Exile and the Kingdom* has never gone out of print, this collection languished until recently in the shadow of Camus's more famous and canonical works, *The Stranger*, *The Fall*, *The Plague*, and *The Myth of Sisyphus*.

Fifty years can erase, enhance, or complicate a writer's reputation and the way his works are read. Albert Camus (1913–60) received the Nobel Prize in 1957, the year *Exile and the Kingdom* was published. By then he was considered a major French writer and intellectual spokesman whose short novels, stories, plays, and essays were—and still are—among the most acute representations of a world without God, of the nature of the human condition without transcendental meaning, and of the existentialist answer to that condition. He also thought of himself—and has often been regarded—as a moralist, setting many of his works in a vague, hallucinatory, and often symbolic place (the Amsterdam of *The Fall*, for instance, or the unnamed town of *The Plague*) that allows the characters' thoughts and ethical dilemmas to occupy the foreground of the reader's attention.

There was a long period during the last fifty years when it was forgotten, especially by Camus's English readers, that in 1957 France, along with its intellectuals, was deeply engaged in the Algerian struggle for independence (1955–62). If Camus continued to be read and admired during this period of forgetting, it was rarely mentioned that as a French Algerian he was anguished, increasingly isolated, and finally silenced in his attempt to advocate a solution—a federation something like England's with its former colonies—that would salvage France's relations with Algeria and still guarantee equal rights for all its citizens.

Camus had condemned colonial injustice as early as the midforties. After a visit to Algeria in 1952, which prompted him to write most of the stories in *Exile and the Kingdom*, he declared in a public letter that the French in North Africa had "the Declaration of the Rights of Man in one hand and a stick for repression in the other." But after all, he was a *pied noir*—the rather derogatory name, meaning "dirty feet," given to the French settlers born in Algeria. His father's family had been there for three generations (his illiterate mother was Italian). They were poor, working-class people, and although they were French nationals, France was at best an abstraction for which his father nevertheless gave his life in the First World War. Among the stories in this volume, "The Voiceless" reflects Camus's intimate understanding of the working poor of French Algeria, and its main character, Yvars, is a barrel maker like Camus's uncle, for whom he worked as an adolescent on his days off from school.

As a young man Camus trained as a teacher, worked as a journalist and theater director, and published poetry and short stories. He contracted tuberculosis, which undermined his health for the rest of his life, but this did not stop him from living and working with a fierce intensity. He went to France in 1940 with the manuscript of *The Stranger* half finished, and it was published to much acclaim in 1942, under the German occupation. He was thirty-one years old.

Camus's early Communist sympathies and his journalism, first in Algeria, then in France writing for the Resistance publication *Combat*, made him a comrade of people like Jean-Paul Sartre and other leftist writers and intellectuals, and an instant enemy of the political right. By the early fifties, however, he had alienated the left too, beginning with his denunciation of Stalinism and followed by his position on Algerian independence, which pleased no one. He was anguished by the terrorism on both sides of the struggle: the torture and massacre of the Arab population by the French and the deliberate killing of French civilians by the Arab militants. He traveled to Algeria in 1956 to try, without success, to broker a civilian truce. Before withdrawing from public debate, in one of his last statements on the subject (after receiving the Nobel Prize), he said: "I believe in justice, but I will defend my mother before justice." Camus was a man of principle, but unlike a good many other French intellectuals, he was not prepared to violate his sense of fundamental human loyalties in the name of an abstract concept.

Above all, he was grief-stricken at the prospect of the expulsion of Algeria's French settlers when France would finally admit defeat and withdraw from its last colonial outpost. He died prematurely in 1960 in an automobile accident, but he felt that the "return" of the *pieds noirs* to metropolitan France—in principle a return to their putative homeland—would mean an exile from the land of their birth, where they were both rooted and rootless, not just another minority but intimate strangers.

Fifty years on, the Algerian war has again become a vital topic in France and in other Western countries as terrorism and its permutations, whether sponsored by nation states, sectarian groups, or independence movements, are once more an urgent concern. Today, long after the demise of France's colonial empire, and especially since the publication in 1994 of Camus's unfinished autobiographical novel *The First Man*, we are in a position to take a fresh look at the stories in *Exile and the Kingdom* (as critics like Conor Cruise O'Brien and David Carroll have begun to do). We can now see more clearly, perhaps, how Algeria and its people—European protagonists, Arab or indigenous Others—are represented in Camus's work, and how this imagined relationship frames the struggles of many of his characters.

The stories that make up *Exile and the Kingdom*—especially but not only those set in North Africa—explore, in a more consciously nuanced way than the novels and plays, the dilemma of the outsider or stranger, and the vexed poles of solitude and community, exile and belonging, speech and silence.

These themes as they play out in "The Guest," for example, come perhaps closest to Camus's own situation during the Algerian struggle for independence. The French title of this story is *L'Hôte*, which means, tellingly, both "host" and "guest." Watching the approach of his two visitors from the top of the plateau where his schoolhouse is situated, the teacher Daru thinks of the destitute families of his Arab students, to whom he distributes extra rations of grain, and of the land they share:

> The country was like that, a cruel place to live, even without the men, who didn't help matters. But Daru had been born here. Anywhere else, he felt exiled.

He becomes host to an Arab prisoner, his "guest" for the night, but there is a sense in which Daru and his people are the true guests in this land, this kingdom of stones and opaque native inhabitants. The ancient rules of hospitality, his sympathies, and principles, prevent him from turning in his prisoner-guest, and—like Camus—from taking sides during this period of unrest. Ultimately he finds himself isolated by both the French colonial community and the rebellious Arabs. His deliberate stance of neutrality is an assertion of the individual against the claims of conflicting communities, each of which sees him as a traitor. But exile and silence are thrust upon him even in the land of his birth.

In this story and the others set in North Africa (and one in South America), an often cruel but beautiful landscape and its indigenous inhabitants play a central role. The sun and sea of Algeria ("The Voiceless"), its cold and hostile desert plateaus, its barren stony plains and glittering nights ("The Adulterous Wife," "The Renegade, or A Confused Mind," "The Guest"), the dark tropical jungle, the river and red dust of Brazil ("The Growing Stone") are evoked with such power and lyricism that these non-European lands themselves seem to possess the characters like an insistent lover.

"The adulterous wife" Janine, for instance, in the story of that title, suddenly finds herself surrounded by proud, dignified Arabs as icy and severe as the remote desert plateau in winter where she accompanies her husband on a business trip. Her first reaction as a French colonial is outrage at the arrogance of these people, having always regarded them, with their alien language and culture, as simply a backdrop to her unfulfilled life. Seeing a nomad encampment, not even the men themselves, she is finally able to imagine them as agents, if in a rather romanticized way:

Since the beginning, on the dry earth of this measureless land scraped to the bone, a few men ceaselessly made their way, possessing nothing but serving no one, the destitute and free lords of a strange kingdom.

In the end, at least for a moment, she opens herself up to this land, which slowly seduces and possesses her. She has a brief glimpse of what it might mean to become truly herself in this place, although she has no words to say it, and to do so she must betray her husband, and through him her people. In her unresolvable inner conflict she embodies the dilemma of mutually exclusive loyalties that asserts itself throughout this collection.

The protagonists of all the stories in *Exile and the Kingdom* are in a way doubly exiled, like Daru and Janine, caught in a conflict between a personal truth—usually bound to their connection with a particular land—and betrayals of various sorts. In "The Voiceless," for example, the lame barrel maker Yvars and his comrades are silenced by their multiple allegiances in the wake of a failed strike. Yvars's passivity and resignation, however, are not so different from Janine's: "he had nothing to do but wait, quietly, without really knowing why." Again, Camus uses the language of love and seduction to indicate Yvars's relation to the landscape:

Mornings when he was heading back to work, he no longer liked looking at the sea, ever faithful to their rendezvous . . .

But what are he and the others waiting for? Perhaps to rise above resignation, to claim their rights as workers and respect for the hard-won competence required by their trade; certainly they are waiting to claim this land ("his country") that should belong to them as much as to the French owning class or to their Arab neighbors. But they are "the mute." Only Marcou, the union representative, has words to express the traditional hostility between union and management, but these words do not begin to express the complexities of their situation.

Their exile in the land of their birth is related to a conflict of loyalties that, on a deeper level, reflects a conflict of civilizations: are they French or Algerian? Can Europeans with roots in the Christian West ever be at home in a land inhabited by North African Arabs and other native peoples with their own indigenous faiths? A man driven mad and literally silenced by the internalized conflict of civilizations and allegiances—his tongue has been cut out—is the narrator and protagonist of "The Renegade, or A Confused Mind." Camus experiments in this story with a monologue voiced, unusually, by a native missionary crazed by the "savage sun" and the "cruelty of the savage inhabitants" he has tried to convert from Fetishism to Christianity in their strange city of salt, but especially by his own multiple betrayals: of his land, his people, his indigenous faith, his adopted faith, and above all himself.

In this and other stories, the exotic and non-European is both demonized and romanticized, and an unbridled and savage sensuality is set in contrast to the inhibited, reason-worshipping culture of the Judeo-Christian West. In "The Growing Stone," the last story in the collection, the French engineer d'Arrast is a voluntary exile who has chosen to leave Europe behind and come to Brazil, to a remote town along the Amazon, in order to build a dam. Camus conceived this story in 1949 during a visit to Brazil—a setting even more exotic than Algeria—and although it is much more realistic, it shares with "The Renegade, or A Confused Mind" a fablelike quality. Like Daru in "The Guest," d'Arrast must choose between the colonists and Europeanized notables, and the destitute, barely Christianized descendants of African slaves. He is beguiled by the land and the seductive vitality of these people—embodied by a beautiful young black girl. And it is only by honoring a poor native who has undertaken a Sisyphean task that d'Arrast is able to honor himself. Like Janine, he experiences a moment of joyous belonging; in this joy, he too betrays his own people.

Only "Jonas, or The Artist at Work," written in 1946, is set in France, but it turns on some of the same themes. Told in the third person by an omniscient and distinctly sardonic narrator, this story skewers the hypocrisy and self-serving vanity of the art world (read: literary world). And of course Camus himself, like the painter Gilbert Jonas, experienced in his personal life the conflict between the commitments to family and others and the commitment to art, which takes time and above all solitude. Like the protagonists in the Algerian stories, Jonas finds himself exiled in his own house, which is filled with unwanted visitors, and he is finally reduced to silence by his inability to be faithful, at all costs, "to his star."

As an artist like Jonas and a French Algerian like Daru, Camus was indeed doubly exiled. He was a writer living in a country whose language was his native tongue, but his homeland, at least as he felt it, was elsewhere. In *Exile and the Kingdom* we can see that he envisioned Algeria as a kind of mythic place, with its harsh beauty and sensual power, in which Europeans, Arabs, and others might possess—and be possessed by—the land together. Yet in these stories, reconciliation between the individual and the community, longing and belonging, speech and silence can only be imperfectly, ruefully imagined but not realized.

Carol Cosman

Exile and the Kingdom

The Adulterous Wife

A fly circled feebly for a moment toward the raised windows of the bus. Oddly, it came and went in silence, in exhausted flight. Janine lost sight of it, then saw it land on her husband's motionless hand. It was cold. The fly trembled at every gust of sandy wind that scratched against the windows. In the meager light of the winter morning, with a great screech of sheet metal and shock absorbers, the vehicle rolled and pitched, scarcely advancing. Janine looked at her husband. With tufts of graying hair sprouting on a low brow, a large nose, an uneven mouth, Marcel looked like a sulky faun. At every bump in the road, she felt him bounce against her. Then he let his torso sink heavily on his spread legs, his eyes glazed, once again inert, absent. Only his thick, hairless hands seemed to move, looking even shorter in the gray flannel that hung below his shirtsleeves and covered his wrists. They squeezed a little canvas case, set between his knees, so tightly that they appeared not to feel the hesitant course of the fly.

Suddenly they heard distinctly the screaming of the wind, and the mineral fog that surrounded the bus became even thicker. The sand now hurled itself at the windows in fistfuls, as if thrown by invisible hands. The fly waved a frail wing, flexed its legs, and flew off. The bus slowed down and seemed about to stop. Then the wind appeared to grow calmer, the fog cleared a little, and the vehicle sped up again. Holes of light were opening in the landscape drowned in dust. Two or three palm trees, delicate and whitened, as though cut from metal, surged at the window only to disappear an instant later.

"What a country!" Marcel said.

The bus was full of Arabs who seemed to be asleep, buried in their burnooses. Some had put their feet up on the benches and swayed more than others with the movement of the vehicle. Their silence, their impassiveness, weighed on Janine; she felt she had been traveling for days with this mute escort. Yet the bus had left at dawn from the railway station, and for two hours in the cold morning it had been advancing over a rocky, desolate plateau that, at least at the outset, had extended its lines straight to the reddening horizon. But the wind had risen, and little by little it had swallowed the vast expanse. From that moment, the passengers could see nothing; one by one they had fallen quiet and had navigated in silence in a kind of sleepless night, sometimes rubbing their lips and eyes, irritated by the sand that had filtered into the car.

"Janine!" She jumped at her husband's summons. She thought once more what a ridiculous name she had, tall and strong as she was. Marcel wanted to know where to find the sample case. She felt around the empty space under the bench with her foot and encountered an object she thought must have been the case. She could not bend down without coughing a little. In high school, though, she was first in gymnastics, never out of breath. Was it so long ago? Twenty-five years. Twenty-five years were nothing; it seemed to her only yesterday that she was hesitating between a free life and marriage, only yesterday that she had felt such anguish at the thought that perhaps one day she would grow old alone. She was not alone, and that law student who never wanted to leave her was now at her side. She had accepted him in the end, although he was a little short and she did not much like his hungry, sudden laugh, or his dark protruding eyes. But she loved his courage to live, which he shared with the French of this country. She also loved his downcast air when events or men belied his expectations. Above all, she loved being loved, and he had flooded her with attentions. Making her feel so often that she existed for him, he made her existence real. No, she was not alone . . .

The bus, with great warning honks, found its way through invisible obstacles. Inside, however, no one moved. Janine suddenly felt that someone was looking at her and turned toward the bench that was the extension of hers, across the aisle. He was not an Arab, and she was surprised not to have noticed him at their departure. He wore the uniform of the French legion of the Sahara and a *kepi* of grayish brown cloth on his tanned face, which was long and pointed like a jackal's. He examined her with his clear eyes, staring silently. She blushed all of a sudden and turned back toward her husband, who continued to gaze before him, into the fog and wind. She wrapped herself up snugly in her coat. But she could still see the French soldier, tall and thin, so thin in his close-fitting tunic that he seemed made of some dry and crumbling matter, a mixture of sand and bone. It was at this moment that she saw the thin hands and sunburned faces of the Arabs in front of her, and she noticed that despite their ample clothing, they seemed to have plenty of room on the benches where she and her husband were barely perched. She pulled the lapels of her coat closer. Yet, she was not so heavy but tall and full, fleshy and still desirable—she certainly felt it in men's gazes—with her rather childish face, her bright, clear eyes in contrast to this big body that was, she knew, warm and welcoming.

No, nothing was the way she had imagined. When Marcel had wanted to take her along on his trip, she had protested. He had pondered this journey for a long time—since the end of the war, to be precise, around the time when commerce had returned to normal. Before the war, the small fabric business he had taken over from his parents, when he had given up his legal studies, had made them a decent living. On the coast, the early years could be happy. But he had not much liked physical effort, and very quickly he had stopped taking her to the beach. The little car took them out of town only for their Sunday drive. The rest of the time, he preferred his shop of multicolored fabrics in the shade of the arcades of this half-native, half-European quarter. They lived above the boutique in three rooms decorated with Arab hangings and middle-class furniture. They had not had children. The years had passed in the shadows they had maintained behind the half-closed shutters. Summer, the beaches, the drives, even the sky were long ago. Nothing but his business seemed to interest Marcel. She believed she had discovered his true passion, which was money, and she did not like this, without exactly knowing why. After all, it was to her advantage. He was not miserly; on the contrary, he was generous, especially with her. "If anything happens to me," he would say, "you'll be protected." And indeed one must be protected from need. But more than that, aside from the simplest needs, where would she find protection? That was what she felt from time to time in a confused way. Meanwhile, she helped Marcel keep his books and occasionally took a turn at the shop. The hardest time was summer, when the heat killed even the sweet sensation of boredom.

Suddenly in midsummer, the war, Marcel mobilized then rejected by the army, the scarcity of fabrics, business at a halt, the streets hot and deserted. If something happened, henceforth she would no longer be protected. That was why, since the return of fabrics to the market, Marcel had imagined traveling to the villages of the high plateaus and the south to bypass the middlemen and sell directly to the Arab merchants. He had wanted to take her with him. She knew that travel

was difficult, she had trouble breathing, she would have preferred to wait for him. But he was obstinate and she had
accepted because it would have taken too much energy to
refuse. Here they were now, and really, nothing was the way
she had imagined. She had feared the heat, the swarms of flies,
the filthy hotels reeking of anise. She had not thought of the
cold, of the cutting wind, of the nearly polar plateaus clut-
tered with moraines. She had also dreamed of palm trees and
soft sand. She saw now that the desert was not that at all but
only stone, stone everywhere, in the sky where, crunching
and cold, the stone dust alone still reigned, as on the earth
where alone, between the stones, the dry grass grew.

The bus stopped abruptly. The driver fired off a few words
in that tongue she had heard all her life without understanding. "What's this?" asked Marcel. The driver, this time in
French, said that sand must have clogged up the carburetor,
and Marcel cursed the country again. The driver laughed
heartily and assured them that it was nothing, that he was
going to clean out the carburetor and then they would be on
their way. He opened the doors, the cold wind rushed into
the car, instantly pelting their faces with a thousand grains of
sand. All the Arabs plunged their noses into their burnooses
and hunched in on themselves. "Close the door!" Marcel
shouted. The driver laughed, coming back toward the doors.
Deliberately, he took some tools from under the dashboard,
then, tiny in the fog, disappeared again toward the front of the
bus without closing the door. Marcel sighed. "You can be sure
he's never seen an engine in his life." "Leave it be!" Janine said.

Suddenly, she started. On the embankment, just next to the bus, stood motionless covered shapes. Beneath the hoods of the burnooses, and behind a rampart of veils, only their eyes could be seen. Mute, appearing out of nowhere, they gazed at the travelers. "Shepherds," Marcel said.

Inside the bus, there was utter silence. All the passengers, heads lowered, seemed to be listening to the voice of the wind, unleashed across these endless plateaus. Janine was suddenly struck by the nearly total absence of luggage. At the railway station, the driver had hoisted their trunk and a few bundles onto the roof. Inside, in the overhead nets, only gnarled sticks and flat baskets could be seen. All these people from the south evidently traveled empty-handed.

But the driver was coming back, ever alert. Only his eyes were laughing above the veil with which he, too, had masked his face. He announced that they were on their way. He closed the doors, the sound of the wind was silenced, and now they could hear the rain of sand on the windows. The engine coughed, then died. With persistent pleading from the ignition, it finally turned over and the driver made it shriek as he pressed on the accelerator. With a great sputtering, the bus resumed its journey. From the ragged mass of shepherds, motionless as ever, a hand was raised, then vanished in the fog behind them. Almost immediately, the vehicle began to bounce on the deteriorating road. Shaken, the Arabs swayed ceaselessly back and forth. Yet Janine felt sleep overtaking her when a little yellow box, filled with licorice drops, materialized before her. The soldier-jackal was smiling at her. She hesitated, helped herself, and thanked him. The jackal pocketed the box and instantly swallowed his smile. Now he was staring straight ahead at the road. Janine turned toward Marcel and saw only the solid back of his neck. He was looking through the windows at the dense fog rising up the crumbling embankment.

They had been on the road for hours, and fatigue had extinguished all life inside the bus when cries resounded from outside. Children in burnooses, twirling like tops, jumping, clapping their hands, were running around the vehicle. The bus was driving down a long street flanked by low houses: they were entering an oasis. The wind continued to blow, but the walls stopped the particles of sand, which no longer obscured the light. The sky, however, remained overcast. Amid the cries, with a great screech of brakes, the bus stopped in front of the adobe arcades of a hotel with dirt-streaked windows. Janine got off and, once in the street, felt unsteady. She glimpsed a graceful yellow minaret above the houses. To her left, the first palm trees of the oasis stood out, and she would have liked to go toward them. But although it was close to noon, the cold was sharp; the wind made her shiver. She turned toward Marcel, and saw the soldier coming to meet her. She expected a smile or greeting. He passed without looking at her and disappeared. As for Marcel, he was busy extricating his trunk of fabrics, a black footlocker perched on the roof of the bus. The driver was the only one occupied with the baggage, and he had already stopped, standing on the roof, holding forth to the circle of burnooses gathered around the bus. Janine, surrounded by faces that seemed carved from leather and bone, besieged by guttural cries, suddenly felt her exhaustion. "I'm going to the hotel," she said to Marcel, who was impatiently shouting at the driver.

She entered the hotel. The manager, a thin and taciturn Frenchman, went before her. He led her up to the first floor, along a gallery facing the street, into a room furnished with only an iron bedstead, a chair painted with white varnish, a wardrobe with no curtains, and behind a rush screen a toilet and sink covered with a fine dusting of sand. When the manager had closed the door, Janine felt the cold coming from the bare whitewashed walls. She did not know where to put down her bag or herself. She had to lie down or remain standing, and in either case to keep shivering. She remained standing, her bag in her hand, staring at a kind of narrow window near the ceiling open onto the sky. She waited but without knowing why. She felt only her solitude and the penetrating cold, and a heavy weight around her heart. She was dreaming, really, almost deaf to the sounds rising from the street punctuated by bursts of Marcel's voice, more aware of the murmur of a river coming from the window, a murmur raised by the wind in the palm trees, so close now, it seemed to her. Then the wind doubled in force, the gentle voice of the waters becoming the whistling of waves. She imagined behind the walls a sea of palm trees, straight and supple, tossing in the storm. Nothing was the way she had imagined, but those invisible waves refreshed her tired eyes. She stood there, heavily, her arms hanging, a little bent, the cold climbing up her heavy legs. She was dreaming of the palm trees, straight and supple, and of the young girl she had been.

After washing up, they went down to the dining room. On the bare walls were paintings of camels and palm trees, drowned in a syrup of pink and violet. The arched windows let in a spare light. Marcel solicited information about the merchants from the hotel owner. Then an old Arab, who bore a military decoration on his tunic, served them. Marcel was preoccupied and tore his bread apart. He stopped his wife from drinking the water. "It's not boiled. Have wine." She did not like that, the wine made her drowsy. And then, there was pork on the menu. "The Koran forbids it. But the Koran didn't know that well-done pork doesn't make people sick. We French, we know how to cook. What are you thinking about?" Janine was thinking of nothing, or perhaps of this cook's triumph over the prophets. But she should hurry. They were leaving again the next morning, heading farther south—he had to see all the important merchants that afternoon. Marcel urged the old Arab to bring the coffee. He nodded his head, without smiling, and edged his way out. "Slowly in the morning, not too quickly in the evening," Marcel said, laughing. The coffee did arrive in the end. They scarcely took time to swallow it and went out into the cold, dusty street. Marcel called a young Arab to help him carry his trunk, but argued on principle about the payment. His opinion, which he declared to Janine yet again, was based on the obscure principle that they always asked double so as to get a fourth.

Ill at ease, Janine followed the two porters. She had put on a wool dress under her heavy coat; she would have liked to take up less space. The pork, though well-done, and the little wine she had drunk, made her somewhat uncomfortable.

They walked through a small park planted with dusty trees. Arabs passed by who stepped aside without appearing to see them, holding the skirts of their burnooses before them. She felt they carried themselves, even dressed in rags, with a kind of pride that the Arabs of her town did not have. Janine followed the trunk, which cut through the crowd and opened a path for her. They passed through a rampart of ocher earth, ending on a little square planted with the same mineral trees and bordered on its far side, wider than the others, by arcades and shops. But they stopped on the square itself, in front of a small structure shaped like an artillery shell, painted a chalky blue. Inside, in the single room lit only by the doorway, behind a plank of gleaming wood, stood an old Arab with a large white mustache. He was serving tea, raising and lowering the teapot above three small, multicolored glasses. Before they could distinguish anything more in the shadows of the shop, the fresh scent of mint tea welcomed Marcel and Janine on the threshold. Hardly through the entrance with its cumbersome garlands of pewter teapots, cups, and plates stacked between racks of postcards, Marcel was standing at the counter. Janine stayed by the doorway. She moved aside so as not to block the light. At that moment, she saw in the dimness behind the old merchant two Arabs looking at her, smiling, seated on the bulging sacks that graced the entire back of the shop. Red and black carpets, embroidered shawls hung on the walls, the ground was crowded with sacks and little cases full of aromatic herbs. On the counter, around a scale with pans of gleaming copper and an old meter stick with worn markings, were stacks of sweet loaves, one of which, swaddled in a large blue paper, was sliced off at the end. The odor of wool and spices floating through the room emerged behind the scent of tea when the old merchant placed the teapot on the counter and greeted them.

Marcel spoke rapidly in that low voice he used when talking business. Then he opened his trunk, displayed his cloths and silks, pushing away the scale and the meter stick in order to spread his wares for the old merchant. He got excited, raised his voice, laughed inanely, like a woman who wants to please and doubts herself. Now, with his hands open, he made the gestures of buying and selling. The old man shook his head, passed the tea platter to the two Arabs behind him, and said only a few words that seemed to discourage Marcel. He gathered up his fabrics and piled them into the trunk, then wiped an improbable sweat from his forehead. He called to the little porter and they set off again toward the arcades. In the first shop, although the merchant had initially affected the same Olympian manner, they were a little more fortunate. "They think they're God himself," Marcel said, "but they do business, too! Life is hard for everyone."

Janine followed without answering. The wind had almost ceased. The sky was clearing in places. A cold, glittering light fell through wells of blue, penetrating the thickness of the clouds. By now they had left the square. They walked through the little streets, along the earthen walls hung with decaying December roses, or here and there a dry, worm-riddled pomegranate. A scent of dust and coffee, the smoke from a bark fire, the odor of stone and sheep, floated through this part of town. The shops, dug into niches in the walls, were far apart. Janine felt her legs growing heavy. But her husband was calming down, he was beginning to sell and was feeling more conciliatory. He called Janine "Baby," and said the trip would not have been for nothing. "Of course not," Janine replied. "It's better to deal with them directly."

They returned by another street toward the center of town. It was late afternoon, the sky was now almost clear. They stopped on the square. Marcel rubbed his hands, looking tenderly toward his trunk. "Look," Janine said. From the other end of the square, a tall Arab was coming toward them; he was thin, vigorous, covered by a sky blue burnoose, shod in supple yellow boots, gloves on his hands, holding his narrow, tanned head high. Only the *chèche* he was wearing wrapped as a turban distinguished him from the French officers of Native Affairs that Janine had sometimes admired. He walked steadily in their direction but seemed to be looking beyond them, slowly drawing off one of his gloves. "Oh well," Marcel remarked, shrugging his shoulders, "there's one who thinks he's a general." Yes, here they all had that proud bearing, but this man really went too far. Although they were surrounded by the empty space of the square, he walked directly toward the trunk without seeing it, without seeing them.

Then the distance separating them suddenly dwindled and the Arab was upon them; Marcel grabbed the handle of the tin case and pulled it behind him. The other man went by, apparently taking no notice, and headed with the same gait toward the ramparts. Janine looked at her husband, who wore his downcast expression. "They think they can get away with anything now," he said. Janine did not answer. She despised the stupid arrogance of this Arab and suddenly felt unhappy. She wanted to leave, she thought about her little apartment. The idea of returning to the hotel, to that icy room was discouraging. She suddenly remembered that the manager had suggested they go up to the roof of the fort, which commanded a view of the desert. She told Marcel, and suggested they could leave the case at the hotel. But he was tired, he wanted to sleep a little before dinner. "Please," Janine said. He looked at her, suddenly attentive. "Of course, my dear," he replied.

She waited in the street in front of the hotel. The crowd, dressed in white, became increasingly numerous. Not a single woman was to be seen, and Janine thought she had never seen so many men. Yet none of them looked at her. Some, without appearing to see her, turned slowly toward her with that tan, thin face that made them all look alike to her, the face of the French soldier in the bus, the Arab with the gloves, a face at once cunning and proud. They turned that face toward the foreign woman, they did not see her, and then, lightly and silently, they passed around her as her ankles swelled. And her

unease, her need to get away, increased. "Why did I come?"
But Marcel was already on his way back.

It was five o'clock in the afternoon when they climbed
the stairway of the fort. The wind had completely died down.
The sky, entirely clear, was now a periwinkle blue. The cold
air, drier than before, stung their cheeks. Halfway up the stairs,
an old Arab lying against the wall asked if they wanted a
guide, but without moving, as if he were certain in advance of
their refusal. The stairway was long and straight, despite several landings of packed earth. As they climbed, the space
expanded and they rose into a light that grew increasingly
vast, cold, and dry, in which each sound from the oasis reached
them with a distinct purity. The illuminated air seemed to
vibrate around them with a vibration that grew longer as they
advanced, as if their passage through the crystalline light were
creating an expanding wave of sound. And as soon as they
reached the roof and their gaze was lost beyond the palm
grove in the vast horizon, it seemed to Janine that the whole
sky rang with a single, brief burst of sound, its echoes gradually filling the space above her, then ceasing abruptly, only to
leave her silent before the limitless expanse.

From east to west her gaze slowly shifted, unobstructed,
along the length of a perfect curve. Below her, the blue and
white roofs of the Arab village overlapped, stained by the
bloodred spots of peppers drying in the sun. There was no
one to be seen, but from the inner courtyards rose a pun-
gent aroma of roasting coffee along with laughing voices and

incomprehensible shufflings. A little farther off, the tops of the palm groves, divided by the clay walls into unequal squares, rustled in a wind that could no longer be felt on the rooftop. Farther still, and as far as the horizon, began the ocher and gray realm of stones, where no life stirred. It was only at some distance from the oasis, near the *wadi* that bordered the palm grove on the west, that large black tents could be distinguished. All around a herd of motionless dromedaries, tiny at this distance against the gray earth, formed the dark signs of a strange writing whose meaning had yet to be deciphered. Above the desert, the silence was immense, like space.

Janine, leaning her whole body against the parapet, was speechless, incapable of tearing herself away from the void opening before her. Beside her, Marcel was agitated. He was cold, he wanted to go back down. What was there to see up here, anyway? But she could not wrest her gaze from the horizon. Down there, farther south, at the place where sky and earth met in a pure line, down there—suddenly it seemed to her that something was waiting that she had not known until today and yet had always longed for. In the advancing afternoon, the light softened gently; the crystalline sharpness dissolved. At the same time, in the heart of a woman brought there by chance alone, a knot tightened by years, habit, and boredom was slowly loosening. She looked at the nomad encampment. She had not even seen the men who were living there, nothing was moving among the black tents, and yet she could think only of them, of their existence, which she had hardly known of until today. Homeless, remote from the world, they were a handful of men wandering through the vast territory her gaze had discovered, and which was nonetheless only a trivial part of a still greater space, whose dizzying course stopped only thousands of kilometers farther south, where the first river finally waters the forest. Since the beginning, on the dry earth of this measureless land scraped to the bone, a few men ceaselessly made their way, possessing nothing but serving no one, the destitute and free lords of a strange kingdom. Janine did not know why this idea filled her with a sadness so sweet and so vast that she closed her eyes. She only knew that this kingdom had been promised to her from time immemorial, and that it would never be hers, never again, except perhaps in that fleeting moment when she opened her eyes once more on the suddenly still sky and its streams of fixed light, as the voices rising from the Arab town fell suddenly quiet. It seemed to her that the turning Earth had simply stopped, and that from now on no one would grow old or die. Everywhere, henceforth, life was suspended, except in her heart, where at that very moment someone was weeping with pain and wonder.

But the light began to move, the cold, clear sun set toward the west, growing slightly pink, while a gray wave took shape in the east, ready to break slowly over the immense expanse. A first dog barked, and his distant call rose in the air, which had grown colder still. Janine realized then that her teeth were chattering. "We'll catch our death," said Marcel, "you're being stupid. Let's go back." But he took her awkwardly by the hand. Docile now, she turned from the parapet and followed him. The old Arab on the stairway, motionless, watched them go down toward the town. She walked blindly, bowed under enormous and sudden exhaustion, dragging her body whose weight seemed unbearable to her. Her exaltation had left her. Now she felt too tall, too heavy, and too white for this world she had just entered. A child, the girl, the dry man, the secretive jackal were the only creatures who could silently tread that earth. What would she do from now on but drag herself into sleep, into death?

She dragged herself, in fact, into the restaurant, with a husband suddenly taciturn or else talking about his fatigue, while she herself struggled weakly against a cold, aware of her mounting fever. Again, she dragged herself to her bed, where Marcel came to join her and quickly turned out the light without further demands. The room was cold as ice. Janine felt the cold overtake her even as her fever rose. She was breathing badly, her blood pulsed without warming her; a kind of fear was growing inside her. She turned over, the old iron bed creaked beneath her weight. No, she did not want to be ill. Her husband was already asleep, she should sleep, too, it was imperative. The stifled sounds of the town reached her through the narrow window. At the Moorish cafés the old phonographs droned out their tunes, which she vaguely recognized, reaching her through the murmur of the idle crowd. She ought to sleep. But she was counting black tents; behind her eyelids motionless camels grazed; vast solitudes wheeled within her. Yes, why had she come? She fell asleep on this question.

A little later she awoke. There was total silence around her. But on the outskirts of town, dogs howled hoarsely in the mute night. Janine shivered. She turned over again, felt her husband's hard shoulder against hers, and all at once, half asleep, nestled against him. She drifted back to sleep, though not deeply, clinging to that shoulder with an unconscious eagerness, as to her safest refuge. She spoke, but she could hardly hear herself. She felt only Marcel's warmth. For more than twenty years, every night, like this, in his warmth, always the two of them, even ill, even traveling, as they were now . . . Besides, what would she have done at home alone? No child! Wasn't that what she was lacking? She did not know. She simply followed Marcel, content to feel that someone needed her. The only joy he gave her was the knowledge that she was needed. He probably did not love her. Love, even hatred, did not have this closed face. But what was its face? They made love at night, without seeing each other, groping in the dark. Was there a love other than one in darkness, a love that would cry out in broad daylight? She did not know, but she knew that Marcel needed her and that she needed this need, that she lived by it day and night, especially at night—each night when he did not want to be alone or grow old or die, with that stubborn expression he assumed and which she some-times recognized on the faces of other men, the only common expression of those madmen who camouflaged themselves as rational beings until delirium caught them and threw them desperately at a woman's body to bury there, undriven by desire, what solitude and the night made them fear.

Marcel shifted a little as if to move away from her. No, he did not love her, he was simply afraid of anything but her, and they should have separated long ago and slept alone until the end. But who can always sleep alone? Only men who are cut off from others by vocation or misfortune, men who lie down every evening with death. But Marcel could never do that, he especially, a weak and helpless child, always frightened by pain, her child, indeed, who needed her and at that very moment gave a kind of groan. She pressed a little closer and placed her hand on his chest. And to herself she called him the pet name she had given him long ago, and which, less and less often now, they used with each other without thinking what they were saying.

She spoke that name with all her heart. She too, after all, needed him, his strength, his little eccentricities, she too was afraid of dying. "If I could overcome this fear, I'd be happy . . ." Very soon, a nameless anguish invaded her. She detached herself from Marcel. No, she could overcome nothing, she was not happy, she was going to die, in fact, without being delivered. Her heart was in pain, she was suffocating under an immense weight, which she suddenly discovered she had been dragging around for twenty years. Now she was struggling under it with all her might. She wanted to be delivered, even if Marcel, even if the others never were! Awake, she sat up in her bed and listened to a call that seemed very near. But from the edges of the night, only the distant and tireless voices of the oasis dogs reached her. A faint wind had risen, in which she heard the gentle waters of the palm groves. It was coming from the south, where the desert and the night mingled now beneath the newly still sky, where life stopped, where no one grew old or died. Then the waters of the wind ran dry and she was no longer even certain of having heard anything except a mute call which, after all, she could readily dismiss or receive, but whose meaning she would never understand unless she answered it at once. At once, yes, that at least was certain!

She rose softly and stood motionless near the bed, attentive to her husband's breathing. Marcel was sleeping. The next moment, the warmth of the bed left her and the cold seized hold. She dressed slowly, groping for her clothes in the faint light coming through the shutters from the street lamps. With her shoes in her hand, she reached the door. Once more she waited a moment in the darkness, then opened it gently. The latch scraped, she stood still. Her heart beat wildly. She listened and, reassured by the silence, again turned the handle. The turning of the latch seemed endless. At last she opened the door, slipped outside, and closed it with the same precautions. Then, with her cheek pressed against the wood, she waited. At the end of a moment, she could hear Marcel's faint breathing. She turned, her face met by the icy night air, and ran the length of the gallery. The hotel door was closed. While she was working the bolt, the night watchman appeared at the top of the stairs with his rumpled face and spoke to her in Arabic. "I'll be back," Janine said, and hurled herself into the night.

Garlands of stars were falling from the black sky above the

palm trees and the houses. She ran along the short avenue, now empty, that led to the fort. The cold, no longer needing to struggle against the sun, had invaded the night; the icy air burned her lungs. But she ran, half-blind, in the darkness. At the end of the avenue, however, lights appeared, then came zigzagging toward her. She stopped, heard a whirring sound, and finally saw behind the advancing lights the enormous burnooses, and under them the fragile bicycle wheels. The burnooses brushed against her; three red lights emerged in the dark behind her and quickly disappeared. She resumed her course toward the fort. Halfway up the stairs, the burning air in her lungs became so sharp she wanted to stop. A final burst hurled her in spite of herself up to the roof, against the parapet that now pressed against her belly. She was breathing hard and everything was swimming before her eyes. Running had not warmed her, she was still trembling all over. But the cold air she swallowed in gulps soon flowed steadily inside her, and a spark of warmth began to glow amidst her shivers. Her eyes opened at last on the spaces of the night.

No breath, no sound, except at times the muffled cracking of stones being reduced to sand by the cold, came to disturb the solitude and silence that surrounded Janine. After a moment, however, it seemed to her that a kind of slow gyration was sweeping the sky above her. In the depths of the dry, cold night thousands of stars were formed unceasingly and their sparkling icicles no sooner detached than they began to slip imperceptibly toward the horizon. Janine could not tear herself away from the contemplation of these shifting fires. She turned with them, and the same stationary progression reunited her little by little with her deepest being, where cold and desire now collided. Before her, the stars were falling one by one, then extinguishing themselves in the stones of the desert, and each time Janine opened a little more to the night. She was breathing deeply, she forgot the cold, the weight of beings, the insane or static life, the long anguish of living and dying. After so many years fleeing from fear, running crazily, uselessly, she was finally coming to a halt. At the same time she seemed to be recovering her roots, and the sap rose anew in her body, which was no longer trembling. Pressing her whole belly against the parapet, leaning toward the wheeling sky, she was only waiting for her pounding heart to settle down, and for the silence to form in her. The last constellations of stars fell in bunches a little lower on the horizon of the desert, and stood motionless. Then, with an unbearable sweetness, the waters of the night began to fill Janine, submerging the cold, rising gradually to the dark center of her being, and overflowing wave upon wave to her moaning mouth. A moment later, the whole sky stretched out above her as she lay with her back against the cold earth.

When Janine returned, using the same precautions, Marcel had not wakened. But he muttered when she lay down, and a few seconds later he suddenly rose. He spoke and she did not understand what he was saying. He stood up and turned on the light, which slapped her full in the face. He walked unsteadily to the sink, and took a long drink from the bottle of mineral water. He was ready to slip back between the sheets when, with one knee on the bed, he looked at her, bewildered. She was weeping uncontrollably, unable to restrain herself. "It's nothing, darling," she said, "it's nothing."

The Renegade,
or A Confused Mind

What a muddle, what a muddle! I must put my head in order. Since they cut out my tongue, another tongue, I don't know, goes on wagging inside my skull, something is talking, or someone, who suddenly shuts up and then begins all over again—oh I hear too many things I'm not saying, what a muddle, and if I open my mouth it's like the noise of rattling pebbles. Some order, any order, says the tongue, and it talks of other things at the same time, yes I always yearned for order. At least one thing is certain, I'm waiting for the missionary who must come to replace me. I'm out here on the track, an hour away from Taghaza, hidden in a pile of rocks, sitting on the old rifle. Day is dawning over the desert, it's still very cold, soon it will be too hot, this land drives you crazy, and I've been here so many years I've lost count . . . No, make an effort! The missionary should arrive this morning or this evening. I've heard he'll come with a guide, maybe they have only a single camel between them. I will wait, I am waiting, the cold, the cold only makes me tremble. Just be patient, filthy slave!

I've been patient so long. When I was at home on the high plateau of the Massif Central, my coarse father, my crude mother, the wine, the lard soup everyday, especially the wine, sour and cold, and the long winter, the glacial wind, the snowdrifts, the disgusting bracken—oh I wanted to go away, to leave them all behind and finally begin to live in the sun, with clear water. I believed the priest, he spoke to me about the seminary and tutored me every day, he had time in that Protestant country where he hugged the walls as he passed through the village. He would talk to me about a future and about the sun, Catholicism is the sun, he used to say, and he taught me to read, he even drilled Latin into my hard head: "Intelligent child, but stubborn as a mule," my skull so hard that all my life, despite all my falls, it never once bled: "Block-head," my pig of a father used to say. At the seminary they were so proud, a recruit from Protestant country was a victory, they saw me arrive like the sun at Austerlitz. A watery sun, it's true, because of the alcohol, they drank sour wine and their children have rotten teeth, *gha gha*, kill the father, that's what one had to do, but no danger that he would throw himself into missionary work since he died long ago, the acidic wine finally ate holes in his stomach, so all that's left is to kill the missionary.

I have a score to settle with him and his masters, with my masters who deceived me, with filthy Europe, they all deceived me. Missionary work, that's all they had to say, go to the savages and tell them: "Here is my Lord, look at him, he never strikes or kills, he commands in a gentle voice, he turns the other cheek, he is the greatest of lords, choose him, see how he made me better, offend me and you'll have proof." Yes, I believed *gha gha* and I felt better, I had fattened up, I was almost handsome, I wanted to be offended. When we walked in tight black rows in the summer under the Grenoble sun and passed girls in light dresses, I did not look away, not me, I despised them, I waited for them to offend me and sometimes they would laugh. Then I would think: "Let them strike me and spit in my face," but their laughter was really just as bad, bristling with teeth and cutting remarks that tore me apart, the offense and the suffering were sweet! My headmaster did not understand when I condemned myself: "Oh no, there *is* good in you!" Good! There was only sour wine in me, that's all, and so even better, for how can a man become better when he is not bad, I had understood that much in everything they taught me. That was the only thing I did understand, a single idea, and intelligent mule that I was, I would take it to its logical conclusion, I sought out penances, I minimized the ordinary, in short I wanted to be an example, me too, so they would notice me, and in noticing me they would pay homage to what had made me better, praise my Lord through me.

Savage sun! It's rising, the desert is changing, it's lost the colour of mountain cyclamens, oh my mountain, and the snow, the sweet soft snow, no, it's a slightly grayish yellow, the thankless hour before the great splendor. Nothing, still nothing all the way to the horizon, down there where the plateau disappears in a circle of still soft colors. Behind me, the track runs back to the dune hiding Taghaza, whose iron name has been beating in my head for so many years. The first to mention it to me was the old, half-blind priest who had retired to the monastery, but why the first, he was the only one, and it was not the city of salt, the white walls in the torrid sun that struck me in his story, no, but the cruelty of the savage inhabitants, and the city closed to all outsiders, except for a single man who had managed to enter, a single man, to his knowledge, had lived to tell what he had seen. They had whipped him and driven him into the desert after putting salt on his wounds and in his mouth, he had met nomads who were compassionate for once, a lucky break, and since then I'd been dreaming about his tale, about the fire of salt and sky, about the house of the fetish and its slaves, could there be anything more barbarous, more exciting, yes, that was my mission, and I had to go and reveal to them my Lord.

At the seminary they plied me with warnings to discourage me and told me that I had to wait, it wasn't missionary country, I was not mature, I had to prepare myself specially, to know who I was, and I still had to be tested, then they would see! But always waiting—oh no—yes, if they liked, for the special preparation and the tests because these were done in

Algeria and they would bring me closer, but as for the rest I shook my hard head and repeated the same thing, to join the most barbarous people and live their life, to show them on their own ground, and even in the house of the fetish, through my example, that the truth of my Lord was strongest. They would offend me, of course, but the offenses did not frighten me, they were essential to the demonstration, and by my endurance I would subjugate those savages, like a powerful sun. *Powerful*, yes, that was the word I kept rolling around on my tongue, I dreamed of absolute power, the kind that forces the adversary to kneel on the ground, to capitulate, that converts him in the end, and the blinder, crueler, more sure of himself he is, wrapped in his conviction, the more his surrender proclaims the royalty of the one who provoked his defeat. Converting decent people who are simply a bit lost, that was our priests' pitiful ideal, I despised them for daring so little with so much power, they had no faith and I did, I wanted to be recognized by the executioners themselves, to cast them on their knees and make them say: "Lord, here is Thy victory," to reign at last with a single word over an army of the wicked. Ah, I was certain of winning that argument, never very sure of myself otherwise, but once I have an idea I will not let it go, that is my strength, yes, my own strength, me, whom they all pitied!

The sun is even higher, my forehead is beginning to burn. The stones around me are quietly cracking, only the barrel of the rifle is still cool, cool like the meadows, like the evening rain, long ago, when the soup was cooking gently, they were waiting for me, my father and my mother, who sometimes smiled at me, perhaps I loved them. But that's all over, a veil of heat is beginning to rise from the track—come on, missionary, I'm waiting for you, now I know the answer to the message, my new masters taught me the lesson, and I know they are right, you must settle accounts with love. When I fled the seminary in Algiers, I imagined them differently, those savages, and only one thing in my daydreams was true: they are wicked. As for me, I'd stolen the money from the bursar's office, left my habit behind, crossed the Atlas Mountains, the high plateaus, and the desert. The driver on the Trans-Saharan line mocked me, too: "Don't go down there"—What were they all going on about?—and the waves of sand for hundreds of kilometers, undulating, advancing then retreating with the wind, and the mountains again, all black peaks and ridges sharp as a blade, and after the mountains we needed a guide to go out on the endless sea of brown stones, shrieking with heat, burning with a thousand mirrors bristling with fire, to that place on the border between the land of the blacks and the country of the whites, where the city of salt stands. And the money the guide stole from me, always naive I had shown it to him, but he left me on the track just near here, after striking me: "Dog, there's the road, the honor is mine, go on down there, they'll teach you," and they taught me, oh yes, they are like the sun that beats down unceasingly except at night, beating fairly and proudly, striking me hard at this very moment, too hard, with the blows of burning lances suddenly thrust from the ground, oh to the shelter, yes to the shelter, under the great rock, before everything gets muddled.

The shade here is good. How can anyone live in the city of salt, in the hollow of that basin full of white heat? On each of the straight walls, rough-hewn by pickaxes, crudely planed, the gashes left by the pickax bristle like dazzling scales, pale scattered sand yellows them a little, except when the wind cleans the straight walls and the terraces, all resplendent then in a searing whiteness under the sky cleansed, too, down to its blue skin. I was blinded in those days when the motionless burning crackled for hours on the surface of the white terraces that seemed joined, as if one day long ago they had all together attacked a mountain of salt, had first flattened it then hollowed out streets, the insides of houses, and windows from the mass, or as if, yes, even better, they had cut out their white and burning hell with a blowtorch of boiling water, just to show that they could live where no one else could, at thirty days' journey from all life, in that hollow in the middle of the desert, where the heat of midday prevents any contact among beings, stands between them and barriers of invisible flame and boiling crystals, where without transition the cold of the night transfixes them one by one in their shells of resin, nocturnal dwellers in a dry ice floe, black Eskimos suddenly shivering in their cubical igloos. Black yes, for they are dressed in long black cloth and the salt that penetrates even under their nails, bitter grit between their teeth in the polar sleep of the nights, the salt they drink in the water from the only spring at the hollow of a shimmering gash, sometimes leaves traces on their dark garments like the tracks of snails after the rain.

Rain, O Lord, one real rain, long hard rain from your sky! Then at last the ghastly city, gradually eaten away, would shrink slowly, irresistibly, and dissolve entirely in a viscous torrent, would bear its ferocious inhabitants toward the sands. One real rain, Lord! But what, which lord, they are the lords! They reign over their sterile houses, over their black slaves who die working in the mines, and each carved-out slab of salt is worth the price of a man in the countries to the south, they pass silently, covered by their veils of mourning in the mineral whiteness of the streets, and come night, when the whole city looks like a milky phantom, they stoop down and enter the shade of the houses where the walls of salt glow dimly. They sleep a weightless sleep, and upon waking they order, they strike, they say that they are a single people, that their god is the true god, and must be obeyed. These are my lords, they know no pity, and like lords they want to be alone, to advance alone, to rule alone, since they alone had the audacity to build a cold torrid city out of salt and sand. And me . . .

What a muddle when the heat rises, I sweat, they never do, now the shade heats up too, I feel the sun on the stone above me, it is striking, striking like a hammer on all the stones and it's the music, the vast music of noon, the vibration of air and stones on the hundreds of kilometers, *gha*, I hear silence as before. Yes, it was the same silence many years ago that welcomed me when the guards led me to them in the

34

sun, in the center of the square, where the concentric terraces rose gradually toward the lid of hard blue sky that rested on the edges of the basin. There I was forced onto my knees in the hollow of this white shield, my eyes eaten by blades of salt and fire coming off all the walls, pale with exhaustion, one ear bloody from the blow the guide had given me, and they, tall and black, looked at me without a word. It was midday. Under the blows of the iron sun, the sky resounded at length, a sheet of metal fired to a white heat, it was the same silence, and they looked at me, time passed, they kept looking at me, and I could not bear their gaze, I was panting harder and harder until at last I wept, and suddenly they turned their backs on me in silence and went off together in the same direction. On my knees all I could see was their feet in the red and black sandals glistening with salt as they lifted the long dark robes, toes slightly turned up, heels lightly striking the ground, and when the square was empty, they dragged me to the house of the fetish.

Crouched, as I am today in the shelter of the rock, and the fire above my head piercing the thickness of the stone, I spent several days in the dark house of the fetish, a little taller than the others, ringed by a wall of salt, but windowless, full of a sparkling night. Several days, and they gave me a bowlful of brackish water and grain, which they threw before me like chicken feed, I gathered it up. By day, the door stayed closed, and yet the darkness became lighter, as if the irresistible sun managed to seep through the masses of salt. No lamp, but feeling my way along I touched garlands of dried palm leaves that decorated the walls, and at the back a small, rough-hewn door whose latch I recognized with my fingertips. Several days, long after—I could not count the days or the hours, but they had thrown me my fistful of grain ten or so times and I had dug a hole for my waste, which I covered each time in vain but the denlike odor remained—long after, yes, the door was opened on its hinges and they entered.

As I crouched in a corner one of them came toward me. I felt the fire of salt against my cheek, I breathed in the scent of palm dust, I watched him come. He stopped a yard away, he stared at me in silence, a sign and I stood up, he stared at me with his shining metallic inexpressive eyes, in his brown horse face, then he raised his hand. Still impassive, he grabbed me by the lower lip, which he slowly twisted until he tore my flesh and without loosening his fingers made me turn around and back up to the center of the room, he pulled on my lip so that I fell to my knees, frantic, my mouth bleeding, then he turned away to rejoin the others standing along the walls. They watched me groaning in the unbearable flame of relentless daylight that entered through the open door, and in that light the sorcerer suddenly appeared with his raffia hair, his torso covered with a breastplate of pearls, his legs bare under a straw skirt, wearing a mask of reeds and wire in which two square openings had been worked for the eyes. He was followed by musicians and women in heavy multicolored robes that showed nothing of their bodies. They danced in front of the small door, but in a crude, barely rhythmic dance, shaking, that's all, and finally the sorcerer opened the small door behind me, the masters did not move, they watched me, I turned around and saw the fetish, his double hatchet-face, his iron nose twisted like a snake.

They brought me before him, at the foot of the pedestal, they made me drink a bitter black water, bitter, and at once my head began to burn, I was laughing, that was the offense, I was offended. They undressed me, shaved my head and body, bathed me in oil, beat my face with ropes soaked in water and salt, and I laughed and turned my head away, but each time two women took me by the ears and held my face up to the sorcerer's blows, I saw only his square eyes, I kept on laughing, covered with blood. They stopped, no one spoke but me, the muddle was already beginning in my head, then they raised me and forced me to look at the fetish, I was not laughing anymore. I knew that I was now sworn to serve him, to worship him, no, I was not laughing anymore, I was choking with fear and pain. And there, in that white house, between those walls scorched outside by the persistent sun, my face turned up, my memory exhausted, yes, I tried to pray to the fetish, there was only him, and even his horrible face was less horrible than the others. It was then that they tied my ankles with a rope the length of my stride, they danced again, but this time in front of the fetish, the masters left one by one.

The door closed behind them, music again, and the sorcerer lit a bark fire and leaped around it, his tall silhouette broke on the angles of the white walls, pulsed on the flat surfaces, filling the room with dancing shadows. He traced a rectangle in a corner where the women dragged me, I felt their dry, soft hands, they placed a bowl of water and a small heap of grain near me and showed me the fetish, I understood that I should keep my eyes fixed on him. Then the sorcerer called them one by one over to the fire, he beat some of them who groaned and then went to prostrate themselves before the fetish my god while the sorcerer kept on dancing, and he made them all leave the room until only one was left, very young, who crouched near the musicians and had not yet been beaten. He took her by a lock of hair, which he twisted tighter and tighter around his fist, she turned over, her eyes bulging, until finally she fell on her back. The sorcerer cried out and let go of her, the musicians turned to the wall, while the square-eyed mask amplified the cry unbearably, and the woman rolled on the ground in a kind of fit and, finally on all fours, her head hidden in her clasped arms, she cried out too, but with a muffled sound, and this was how, still scream- ing and looking at the fetish, the sorcerer took her quickly, viciously, the woman's face invisible now, shrouded under the heavy folds of her robe. And I, alone and lost, I cried out to the fetish too, yes, screamed horror-stricken until a kick landed me against the wall, chewing salt as I am chewing rock today, with my tongueless mouth, waiting for the one I must kill.

Now the sun has just passed the middle of the sky. Through the slits in the rock I see the hole it makes in the overheated metal of the sky, a talkative mouth like mine, that vomits unfettered rivers of flames over the colorless desert. On the track in front of me, nothing, not even dust on the horizon, behind me they must be searching for me, no, not yet, it was only late in the afternoon that they opened the door and I could go out a little, after spending all day cleaning the house of the fetish, renewing the offerings, and in the evening the ceremony would begin in which I was sometimes beaten, sometimes not, but always I served the fetish, the fetish whose image is engraved in iron on my memory and now in my hope. Never had a god so possessed me or enslaved me, my whole life day and night was devoted to him, and pain and the absence of pain—wasn't that joy?—were owing to him and even, yes, desire, by dint of witnessing almost every day that impersonal and vicious act that I heard without seeing, since now I had to face the wall or get beaten. But with my face stuck against the salt, dominated by the bestial shadows that gyrated on the wall, I listened to the long scream, my throat was dry, a burning sexless desire gripped my temples and my belly. So the days followed one another, I could hardly distinguish between them, as if they were liquefying in the torrid heat and the insidious reverberation from the walls of salt, time was no more than a formless lapping in which only cries of pain or possession burst out at regular intervals, a long ageless day in which the fetish reigned like this ferocious sun over my house of rocks, and now as then I weep with unhappiness and desire, a wicked hope burns me, I want to betray, I lick the barrel of my rifle and its soul inside, its soul, only rifles have souls—oh yes, the day they cut out my tongue I learned to worship the immortal soul of hatred!

What a muddle, what a rage, *gha gha*, drunk with heat and anger, lying prostrate on my rifle. Who is gasping here? I cannot bear this endless heat, this waiting, I must kill him. No bird, no blade of grass, stone, an arid desire, silence, their cries, this tongue inside me talking and since they mutilated me the long, flat lifeless suffering, deprived even of the water of the night, the night I was dreaming of, locked in with the god, in my den of salt. The night alone, with its cool stars and its dark fountains could save me, carry me away at last from the wicked gods of men, but always locked in I could not contemplate it. If the other one is late enough, at least I will see the night rise up from the desert and invade the sky, cold vine of gold that will hang from the dark zenith and where I shall drink at leisure, moisten this black and desiccated hole that no muscle of living and supple flesh refreshes now, shall at last forget that day when madness took me by the tongue.

How hot it was, hot, the salt was melting, or so it seemed, the air was eating away my eyes, and the sorcerer entered without his mask. Almost naked under a grayish rag, a new woman followed him whose face, covered by a tattoo that gave her the mask of the fetish, expressed nothing but the idol's malevolent stupor. Her body was slim and flat, alive, and fell at the feet of the god when the sorcerer opened the door of the niche. Then he left without looking at me, the heat rose, I didn't move, the fetish contemplated me over that motionless body whose muscles shifted gently and the woman's idol face didn't change when I approached. Only her eyes grew wider staring at me, my feet touched hers, the heat then began to shriek, and the idol woman, without saying a word, always gazing at me with her dilated eyes, gradually turned onto her back, slowly brought her legs up and raised them as she gently separated her knees. But just then, *gha*, the sorcerer caught me, they all entered and pulled me from the woman, beat me mercilessly on the sinful place, the sin what sin, I'm laughing, where is it, where is virtue, they pinned me against a wall, a steel hand gripped my jaws, another opened my mouth pulled my tongue until it bled, was it me screaming with that bestial cry, a cutting and cool caress, yes cool at last, passed over my tongue. When I regained consciousness I was alone in the night, glued to the wall, covered with hardened blood, a gag of dried, strange-smelling grasses filled my mouth, it was no longer bleeding but it was vacant, and in that absence lived only a tormenting pain. I wanted to get up, I fell back again, happy, desperately happy to die at last, death too is cool and its shade shelters no god.

I did not die, a budding hatred stood up one day, just as I did, walked toward the back door, opened it, and closed it behind me. I hated my people, the fetish was there, and in the depths of the hole in which I found myself, I did more than pray, I believed in him and denied all that I had believed until then. Hail, he was strength and power, he could be destroyed but not converted, he stared over my head with his empty, rusty eyes. Hail, he was the master, the only lord, whose indisputable attribute was malice, there are no good masters. For the first time, rife with offenses, my whole body crying out with a single pain, I surrendered to him and condoned his

41

malignant order, I worshipped in him the principle of wickedness in the world. A prisoner of his kingdom, the sterile city sculpted from a mountain of salt, separated from nature, deprived of the rare and fleeting blooms of the desert, shielded from those chance or affectionate gestures—an unusual cloud a brief and raging rain—known even by the sun or the sands, the city of order, finally, right angles, square rooms, stiff men, I freely became its hating and tortured citizen, I renounced the long history they had taught me. They had deceived me, only the reign of wickedness was seamless, they had deceived me, truth is square, heavy, dense, it does not admit nuance, the good is a daydream, a project endlessly proposed and pursued with exhausting effort, a limit never reached, its reign is impossible. Only evil can go to the limit and reign absolutely, it must be served in order to establish its visible kingdom, then we shall see, then we shall see what it means, only evil is present—down with Europe, reason and honor and the cross. Yes, I converted to the religion of my masters, yes yes I was a slave, but if I too am wicked, I am no longer a slave, despite my hobbled feet and my mute mouth. Oh this heat is driving me crazy, the desert cries out everywhere under the unbearable light, and him, the other, the Lord of gentleness, whose very name revolts me, I deny him, for I know him now. He dreamed and he wanted to lie, they cut out his tongue so that his speech should no longer deceive the world, they pierced him with nails, even his head, his poor head, like mine now, what a muddle, how tired I am, and the earth did not tremble, I'm sure of it, it was not a righteous

man they had killed, I refuse to believe it, there are no righteous men but wicked masters who established the reign of the
implacable truth. Yes, the fetish alone has power, he is the only
god of this world, and hatred is his commandment, the source
of all life, cool water, cool like the mint that chills the mouth
and burns the stomach.

I changed then, they understood, I kissed their hands
when I met them, I was theirs, admiring them tirelessly, I
trusted them, I hoped they would mutilate my people as they
had mutilated me. And when I learned that the missionary
was coming, I knew what I had to do. That day was like the
others, the same blinding day that had gone on so long! Late
in the afternoon we saw a guard appear, running along the
edge of the basin, and a few minutes later I was dragged to the
house of the fetish and the door closed. One of them held me
down in the dark, under the threat of his cross-shaped saber
and the silence lasted a long time until a strange sound filled
the usually peaceful city, voices, which took me a long time to
recognize because they were speaking my language, but when
they rang out the point of the blade was lowered over my
eyes, my guard stared at me in silence. Two voices that I still
hear then drew closer, one asking why this house was guarded
and whether they should break the door in, my lieutenant,
the other said sharply, "No," then added after a moment that
an agreement had been reached that the city would accept a
garrison of twenty men on the condition that they camp outside the walls and respect the customs. The soldier laughed,
they're giving up, eh? But the officer didn't know, in any case

43

they agreed for the first time to receive someone to care for the children and that would be the chaplain, later on they would worry about the territory. The other said that they would cut off the chaplain's you-know-what if the soldiers were not there: "Oh no," the officer replied, "and even Father Beffort will arrive before the garrison, he'll be here in two days." I heard nothing more, lying motionless, flattened under the blade, I was sick, a wheel of knives and needles was churning inside me. They were crazy, they were crazy, they were allowing someone to lay hands on the city, their invincible power, the true god, and the other, the one who was coming, they would not cut out his tongue, he would make a show of his insolent goodness without paying for it, without enduring any offenses. The reign of evil would be postponed, there would still be doubt, they would waste more time dreaming of the impossible good, exhausting themselves in sterile efforts instead of hastening the coming of the only possible kingdom and I was watching the menacing blade, O power that alone reigns over the world! O power, and the city was gradually emptied of its sounds, the door was opened at last, I remained alone, burned, bitter, with the fetish, and I swore to him to save my new faith, my true masters, my despotic god, to betray well, whatever it cost me.

Gha, the heat is subsiding a bit, the stone has stopped vibrating, I can leave my hole, watch the desert as it is covered in turn with yellow and ocher, soon violet. That night I waited for them to sleep, I had jammed the lock on the door, I left with the same step as always, constrained by the rope, I knew the streets, I knew where to find the old rifle, which gate was not guarded, and I arrived here at the hour when the night is fading around a handful of stars while the desert grows a little darker. And now it seems days and days since I've been hiding in these rocks. Quickly, quickly, oh, let him come quickly! In a moment they will start looking for me, they will fly along the tracks from all sides, they won't know that I left for them and to serve them better, my legs are weak, drunk with hunger and hatred. Oh, oh down there, *gha gha*, at the end of the track two camels grow larger, ambling along, already doubled by the short shadows, they run in that vivid and dreamy way they always have. Here they are at last, here they are!

The rifle, quick, and I load it quickly. O fetish, my god down there, may your power be sustained, may the offense be multiplied, may hatred reign mercilessly over a world of the damned, may the wicked be masters forever, may the kingdom come at last where in a single city of salt and iron black tyrants will enslave and possess without pity! And now, *gha gha*, fire on pity, fire on powerlessness and its charity, fire on all that delays the coming of evil, fire twice, and there they go toppling over, falling, and the camels flee straight toward the horizon where a geyser of black birds has just risen in the unchanged sky. I laugh, I laugh, he twists in his hateful habit, he raises his head a little, sees me, me, his hobbled all-powerful master, why is he smiling at me, I am crushing that smile! How good is the sound of the rifle butt in the face of goodness, today, today at last, all is consummated and everywhere in the desert, even hours away, the jackals sniff the absent wind, then start on their way at a patient little trot toward the carrion feast that awaits them. Victory! I raise my arms toward the tender sky, a violet shadow rims its farthest edge, oh Europe's nights, homeland, childhood, why must I weep at the moment of triumph?

He moved, no the sound is coming from somewhere else, and from the other side down there, it's them, here they come, rushing like a flight of dark birds, my masters, who charge at me, grab me, ah ah! Yes, go on, strike, they fear their city sacked and shrieking, they fear the avenging soldiers I have summoned, as they had to be, to the sacred city. Defend yourselves now, strike, strike me first, you possess the truth! Oh my masters, they will conquer the soldiers then, they will conquer the word and love, they will rise up from the deserts, cross the seas, fill the light of Europe with their black veils, strike the belly, yes, strike the eyes, sow their salt on the continent, all vegetation, all youth will be extinguished, and mute hordes with hobbled feet will make their way beside me in the desert of the world under the cruel sun of the true faith, I will no longer be alone. Ah! Pain, the pain they cause me, their rage is good and on this warrior's saddle where they're now quartering me, pity, I am laughing, I love the blow that nails me, crucified.

How silent the desert is! Already night and I am alone, I am thirsty. Waiting still, where is the city, those distant sounds, and the soldiers perhaps victorious, no it can't be, even if the soldiers are victorious they are not wicked enough, they will not know how to reign, they will still insist we must be better, and still millions of men between evil and good, torn, stunned, O fetish why hast thou forsaken me? It's all over, I'm thirsty, my body is burning, a darker night fills my eyes.

This long this long dream, I awaken, but no, I am going to die, the dawn is breaking, the first light of day for other living creatures, and for me the inexorable sun, the flies. Who is speaking, no one, the sky does not part, no, no, God does not speak in the desert, then what is the source of this voice saying: "If you consent to die for hatred and power, who will forgive us?" Is it another tongue inside me or still that other one who refuses to die at my feet, repeating: "Courage, courage, courage"? Ah! What if I were mistaken again! Fraternal men in other times, last resort, O solitude, do not forsake me! Here, here, who are you, torn apart, mouth bleeding, it is you, sorcerer, the soldiers defeated you, the salt is burning over there, it is you my beloved master! Leave behind that face of hatred, be good now, we were mistaken, we shall begin again, we will rebuild the city of God's mercy, I want to go home. Yes, help me, that's it, hold out your hand, give . . .

A fistful of salt fills the mouth of the babbling slave.

The Voiceless

It was midwinter and yet a radiant day was rising on the already bustling town. At the end of the jetty the sea and the sky mingled in a single burst. Yvars, however, took no notice. He was cycling heavily along the boulevards closest to the port. His game leg rested, motionless, on the bicycle's fixed pedal while the other struggled to subdue the paving still damp from the nightly humidity. Without raising his head, barely on his seat, he avoided the tracks of the former tramway, moving aside with an abrupt swerve of the handlebars to let the cars pass that were overtaking him, and from time to time he elbowed the bag slung over his shoulder in which Fernande had put his lunch. Then he would think bitterly about the contents of the bag. Between two slices of thick bread, instead of the Spanish omelet he liked, or a little steak fried in oil, there was only cheese.

The road to the workshop had never seemed so long. And he was getting old. At forty, and although he was still dry like the branch of a vine, his muscles didn't warm up as quickly. Sometimes, reading the sports pages in which a thirty-year-old athlete was called a veteran, he would shrug his shoulders. "If he's a veteran," he would say to Fernande, "then I'm already done for." Yet he knew that the journalist was not entirely wrong. At thirty, your breath was already flagging imperceptibly. At forty, you aren't done for, no, but you're preparing for it in advance. Wasn't that why it had been a long time since he'd looked at the sea as he pedaled to the other end of town, where the barrel works were located? When he was twenty, he never tired of gazing at it—it once held the promise of a happy weekend at the beach. In spite or because of his lameness, he had always loved swimming. Then the years had passed, there was Fernande, the birth of the boy, and to make ends meet, extra hours at the barrel works on Saturdays, on Sundays fixing things for private customers. He had gradually lost the habit of those violent days that were once so satisfying. The deep clear water, the strong sun, the girls, the life of the body, in his country there was no other happiness. And that happiness passed with youth. Yvars continued to love the sea, but only at the end of the day, when the waters of the bay darkened a little. That moment was sweet on the terrace of his house, where he would sit after work, content in his clean shirt, which Fernande knew how to iron just so, and a glass of anisette cloudy with condensation. Evening would come, the sky briefly suffused with softness, and the neighbors talking with Yvars would suddenly lower their voices. He did not know, then, whether he was happy or whether he wanted to cry. At least he was in harmony with those moments, he had nothing to do but wait, quietly, without really knowing why.

Mornings when he was heading back to work, he no longer liked looking at the sea, ever faithful to their rendezvous, but in the evening he would see it again. That morning he was cycling, his head down, hanging more heavily than usual: his heart was heavy, too. When he had gone home from the meeting the evening before, and had announced that they were going back to work, Fernande had said joyfully: "So, the boss is giving you a raise?" The boss was not giving any raises, the strike had failed. They had miscalculated, they had to admit. A strike in anger, and the union had been right not to back them more vigorously. Besides, fifteen workers weren't very important; the union handled other barrel works that had not walked out. They couldn't feel too resentful. The barrel works, threatened by the construction of seagoing tankers and tanker trucks, were not in a strong position. They were making fewer and fewer barrels and wine casks; mostly they were repairing the huge vats already made. The bosses saw their business shrinking, true, but they still wanted to preserve a margin of profit. They still thought the simplest thing was to freeze salaries in spite of the rise in prices. What could the barrel makers do when the works went under? A man doesn't change trades when he's taken the trouble to learn one, and a difficult one, demanding a long apprenticeship. The good barrel maker who adjusted his curved staves, sealed them almost hermetically with fire and an iron hoop, without using straw or tar, was rare. Yvars knew how to do that and he was proud of it. To change trades is nothing, but to renounce what you know, what you've mastered, is not so easy. With a fine trade but no work, you were backed into a corner and just had to resign yourself. But resignation wasn't so easy either. It was difficult to close your mouth, not argue, and keep taking the same route every morning with increasing fatigue, and at the end of the week receive only what they deigned to give you, which was increasingly inadequate.

Then, they had gotten angry. There were two or three who were hesitating, but anger had won them over too after the first discussions with the boss. He had said, in effect, quite drily, that it was take it or leave it. A man doesn't talk that way. "What does he think!" Esposito had said, "That we're going to kiss his feet?" The boss wasn't a bad sort, really. He had taken over from his father, had grown up in the workshop, and had known almost all the workers for thirty years. He sometimes invited them for a bite to eat at the barrel works; they would grill sardines or sausage on the fire made of shavings, and with the help of a little wine he was really very decent. At the New Year he always gave five bottles of wine to each of the workers, and often, when there was illness or simply an important event—a wedding or a communion—he made them a gift of money. At the birth of his daughter, there had been sugar-coated almonds for everyone. Two or three times he had invited Yvars to hunt on his property down the coast. He certainly cared for his workers, and he often recalled that his father had begun as an apprentice. But he had never gone to their homes, he did not understand. He thought only of himself because he knew only himself, and now it was take it or leave it. In other words, he had turned stubborn. But of course he could allow himself to be.

They had forced the union's hand, the workshop had closed its doors. "Don't wear yourselves out on picket lines," the boss had said. "When the workshop isn't operating, I save money." This was not true, but it hadn't helped matters since he was telling them to their faces that he only gave them work out of charity. Esposito was in a rage and had told him that he wasn't a real man. The boss was so hot under the collar they'd had to be separated. But at the same time the workers had been impressed. Twenty days on strike, the wives at home looking sad, two or three of them discouraged, and in the end the union had advised them to give in with the promise of arbitration and the compensation of additional hours for the days missed on strike. They had decided to go back to work. By bluffing, of course, by saying that it wasn't a done deal, they would see. But that morning, a fatigue that seemed like the weight of defeat, cheese instead of meat, and the illusion was no longer possible. The sun was shining, for all the good it did, the sea held no more promise. Yvars was leaning on his only pedal, and at each turn of the wheel he felt a little older. He could not think of the workshop, of his comrades, and the boss he was going to see again, without his heart sinking a little more. Fernande was worried: "What are you going to say to him?"—"Nothing." Yvars had mounted his bicycle, shaking his head. He clenched his teeth; his small brown, wrinkled face with its delicate features was closed. "A man works. That's enough." Now he was cycling, his teeth still clenched, with a sad, dry anger that darkened everything, even the sky itself.

He left the boulevard and the sea, and entered the damp streets of the old Spanish quarter. They led to a zone occupied only by sheds, scrap-iron warehouses, and garages, where the workshop stood—it was a kind of shed, with masonry walls halfway up, then industrial windows as high as the corrugated tin roof. This workshop looked out over the former barrel works, a court enclosed by an old covered exercise yard that had been abandoned when the enterprise had grown and was now just a storage space for worn out machinery and old barrels. Beyond the court, separated from it by a sort of path covered with old tiles, the boss's garden began, and his house stood at the other end. It was big and ugly but welcoming because of its new vine and the meager honeysuckle that surrounded the outer staircase.

Yvars saw at once that the doors of the workshop were closed. A group of workers was standing silently before them. Since he had worked here, this was the first time he'd found the doors closed on arrival. The boss had wanted to rub their noses in it. Yvars turned to the left, parked his bicycle under the overhang that extended the shed on this side, and walked toward the door. From a distance he recognized Esposito, a tall sturdy fellow, dark and hairy, who worked beside him;

Marcou, the union delegate, with his counter tenor; Said, the only Arab in the workshop; then all the others who silently watched him come. But before he could join them, they suddenly turned toward the doors of the workshop, which were just opening. Ballester, the foreman, appeared in the entrance. He opened one of the heavy doors and then, turning his back on the workers, pushed it slowly on its cast-iron rail.

Ballester, who was the oldest of them all, disapproved of the strike, but he'd kept quiet from the moment Esposito had told him that he was pandering to the boss's interests. Now, he stood near the door, broad and short in his navy blue jersey, already barefoot (apart from Said, he was the only one who worked barefoot), and he watched them enter one by one with his eyes so clear that they seemed colorless in his old sunburned face, his sad mouth under a thick, drooping mustache. They were quiet, humiliated by this defeated entrance, furious at their own silence but less and less able to break it the longer it went on. They passed Ballester without looking at him, knowing that he was executing an order by letting them in this way; his bitter and doleful expression told them what he was thinking. Yvars looked at him. Ballester, who liked him, nodded his head without saying anything.

Now they were all in the little cloakroom to the right of the entrance: open cubicles separated by white wood boards, where a little cupboard had been hung that closed with a key; the last cubicle from the entrance, where it joined the walls of the shed, had been transformed into a shower room above a gutter hollowed out of the clay floor. At the center of the shed, in the various work spaces, were big wine casks already finished but loosely hooped, waiting for the forcing fire, thick benches hollowed with a long groove (and in some of them, circular wooden bottoms had been slipped, waiting to be sharpened at the edges by the adze), and finally blackened fires. Along the wall to the left of the entrance stood the worktables. In front of them, the staves ready for planing were heaped in piles. Along the right-hand wall, not far from the cloakroom, two big, well-oiled mechanical saws glistened, strong and silent.

For a long time now the shed had been too big for the handful of men who occupied it. It was an advantage during heat waves, an inconvenience in winter. But today in that big space, the work standing there, the defective barrels in the corners with the single hoop circling the feet of the staves that opened above like crude wooden flowers, the sawdust that covered the benches, the boxes of tools, and the machines— all this made the workshop seem abandoned. They looked at it, clothed now in their old jerseys, in their faded and patched trousers, and they hesitated. Ballester was observing them. "Okay," he said. "Let's get going." One by one they found their places without saying anything. Ballester was going from one post to the other and giving a brief rundown on the work to be started or finished. No one answered. Soon the first hammer resounded against the corner of iron-rimmed wood that dug a circle on the swollen middle of the barrel, an adze whined in a nest of wood, and one of the saws, handled by Esposito, started up with a loud noise of straining blades.

Said, when asked, carried staves or lit the fires of shavings on which they placed the barrels to make them swell in their corset of iron-tipped blades. When no one claimed him, he would go to the worktables and rivet the big rusty hoops together with powerful hammer blows. The odor of burned shavings was beginning to fill the shed. Yvars, who was planing and adjusting the staves shaped by Esposito, recognized the old perfume and his heart ached a little. Everyone was working in silence, but warmth, life, was gradually revived in the workshop. Through the large industrial windows a fresh light filled the shed. The smoke rose bluish in the golden air; Yvars even heard an insect buzzing nearby.

At this moment the door leading out to the old barrel works opened at the back wall, and M. Lassalle, the boss, stopped on the threshold. Thin and dark, he was hardly more than thirty years old. His white shirt was open on a beige gabardine suit, his physical presence was easy and self-confident. In spite of his bony face, cut like the blade of a knife, he generally inspired sympathy, like most people whose attitudes have been freed by playing sports. Yet he seemed a little embarrassed coming in the door. His greeting was less hearty than usual; in any case, no one answered it. The noise of the hammers paused, a little out of tune, and resumed more harmoniously. M. Lassalle took a few indecisive steps, then he came forward toward little Valery, who had been working with them for only a year. Near the mechanical saw, a few steps away from Yvars, he was placing a bottom on a wine cask, and the boss watched him do it. Valery continued to work without saying anything. "So then, son," said M. Lassalle, "everything all right?" The young man suddenly became more awkward in his movements. He glanced at Esposito who, beside him, was gathering a pile of staves in his enormous arms to carry to Yvars. Esposito was looking at him, too, even as he continued his work, and Valery stuck his nose in his wine cask without answering the boss. Lassalle, a bit dumbfounded, remained standing for a moment in front of the young man, then shrugged his shoulders and turned toward Marcou. The worker was sitting astride his bench, and with small, slow, precise blows was almost finished sharpening the edge of a bottom. "Good morning, Marcou," Lassalle said, in a drier tone. Marcou did not answer, attentive only to taking very thin shavings from his wood. "What are you up to?" said Lassalle in a loud voice, this time turning toward the other workers. "We don't agree, okay. But we still have to work together. So what's the point? What good does this do?" Marcou stood up, lifted his bottom piece, verified the circular edge with the flat of his hand, squinted his mournful eyes with an air of great satisfaction, and, still silent, headed toward another worker who was assembling a wine cask. Throughout the workshop, only the sound of the hammers and the mechanical saw could be heard. "Fine," said Lassalle, "when you've gotten over this, let me know through Ballester." He walked calmly out of the workshop.

Almost immediately afterward, above the din, a bell rang twice. Ballester, who had just sat down to roll a cigarette, got up heavily and went to the little back door. After his departure, the hammers struck less forcefully; one of the workers had even stopped when Ballester returned. From the door he said only: "The boss is asking for you, Marcou and Yvars." Yvars's first movement was to go and wash his hands, but Marcou grabbed him by the arm as he passed and he followed the other man, limping out.

Outside in the courtyard, the light was so fresh, so liquid, that Yvars felt it on his face and his bare arms. They struggled up the outside staircase under the honeysuckle, already blooming with a few flowers. When they entered the hallway hung with diplomas, they heard the child crying and M. Lassalle's voice saying: "You'll lie down after lunch. We'll call the doctor if it doesn't feel better." Then the boss burst into the hallway and ushered them into the little office that was already familiar to them, furnished in fake country style, the walls decorated with athletic trophies. "Sit down," Lassalle said, taking the place behind his desk. They remained standing. "I asked you to come because you, Marcou, are the union delegate, and Yvars, you're my oldest employee after Ballester. I don't want to resume the discussions that are over now. I cannot, absolutely cannot, give you what you ask. The matter's been settled, we've concluded that everyone should go back to work. I see that you're resentful, and that's painful to me, I'll tell you straight. I simply want to add this: what I cannot do today, I may be able to do when business picks up again. And if I can do it, I will do it even before you ask me to. In the meantime, let's work together in peace." He was quiet, seemed to reflect, then raised his eyes to them.

"Okay?" he said. Marcou was gazing outside. Yvars, his teeth clenched, wanted to speak but could not. "Listen," Lassalle said, "you're all stubborn. That will pass. But when you're reasonable again, don't forget what I've just said." He stood up, came toward Marcou, and held out his hand. "Ciao!" he said. Marcou suddenly blanched, his charming singer's face hardened, and in the space of a second grew mean. Then he turned abruptly on his heels and left. Lassalle, blanching too, looked at Yvars without holding out his hand. "You can all go to Hell!" he cried.

When they returned to the workshop, the workers were breaking for lunch. Ballester had gone out. Marcou said only, "Hot air," and he went back to his work space. Esposito stopped biting into his bread to ask what they had answered; Yvars said they hadn't. Then he went to find his bag and came back to sit on the bench where he was working. He was beginning to eat when, not far from him, he saw Said, lying on his back in a heap of shavings, gazing dreamily toward the panes of glass, now tinted blue in the fading light. He asked if he'd already finished. Said said he had eaten his figs. Yvars stopped eating. His feeling of uneasiness since the interview with Lassalle suddenly disappeared, leaving in its place only a fine warmth. He stood up, breaking his bread, and said at Said's refusal that next week would be better. "You'll invite me then," he said. Said smiled. Now he was biting into a piece of Yvars's sandwich, but delicately, like a man who wasn't hungry.

Esposito took an old pot and lit a little fire of wood shavings. He set about reheating some coffee he'd brought in a bottle. He said that it was a gift to the workshop from his grocer, who had given it to him when he had learned about the failure of the strike. A mustard jar was passed from hand to hand. Each time Esposito poured the presugared coffee, Said swallowed it with more pleasure than he'd shown eating. Esposito drank the remains of the coffee from the burning pot, smacking his lips and cursing. Just then, Ballester entered to announce it was time to go back to work.

While they were getting up and putting papers and dishes into their bags, Ballester came to stand among them and suddenly said that it was a hard blow for everyone, and for him too, but that was no reason to behave like children, it did no good to sulk. Esposito, pot in hand, turned toward him; his long, meaty face had reddened all at once. Yvars knew what he was going to say, and that everyone was thinking at the same time that he, that they, were not sulking, that they had shut their mouths, it was take it or leave it, and that anger and impotence sometimes caused such pain you couldn't even cry out. They were men, that's all, and they were not about to go around smiling and simpering. But Esposito said nothing of this, his face finally relaxed, and he gently clapped Ballester on the shoulder while the others returned to their work. Once again the hammers pounded, the large shed filled with the familiar din, with the odor of shavings and old clothes damp with sweat. The big saw throbbed and bit into the fresh wood of the stave that Esposito was slowly pushing in front of him. Where it bit, dampened sawdust sprayed out and covered the rough, hairy hands firmly holding the wood on each side of the roaring blade with something like breadcrumbs. When the stave was cut, they no longer heard the noise of the motor.

Leaning over the plane, Yvars now felt the ache in his back. Usually, fatigue came only later. Clearly, he had lost his stamina during the weeks of inaction. But he was also thinking that age makes working with your hands harder, that work becomes more than simple precision. That ache was also the first sign of old age. Where the muscles are at play, work in the end is a curse, it precedes death and evenings of great effort, sleep is truly like death. The boy wanted to be a teacher, he was right, those who made big speeches about manual labor did not know what they were talking about.

When Yvars straightened up for a breather and also to chase away these gloomy thoughts, the bell rang again. It was insistent, but in such an odd way, with short intervals between imperious repetitions, that the workers stopped. Ballester was listening, surprised, then made up his mind and went slowly to the door. He had disappeared for a few seconds when the ringing finally ceased. They went back to work. Again, the door was shoved open and Ballester ran toward the cloak-room. He came out, shod in his espadrilles, pulling on his jacket, and said to Yvars in passing, "The girl had an attack. I'm going to fetch Germain," and ran toward the big door. Doctor Germain was on call for the workshop; he lived in the neighborhood. Yvars repeated the news without comment. They stood around him and looked at each other, embarrassed. Soon they heard only the motor of the mechanical saw spinning freely. "Perhaps it's nothing," one of them said. They took their places again, the workshop was filled once more with their noises, but they worked slowly, as if they were expecting something.

A quarter of an hour later, Ballester entered once more, hung up his jacket, and without saying a word left again by the back door. On the glass walls, the light wasn't quite as bright. A little later, in the intervals when the saw was not biting into the wood, they heard the dull siren of an ambulance, at first far off, then close by, now silent. After a moment Ballester came back and they all went over to him. Esposito had cut the motor. Ballester said that while undressing in her room, the child had suddenly fallen, as if she'd been cut down. "So that's it!" Marcou said. Ballester nodded his head and gestured vaguely toward the workshop, but he looked stunned. Once again they heard the ambulance siren. They were all there, in the silent workshop, under the waves of yellow light dispersed by the glass walls, with their rough, useless hands hanging down by their old trousers covered with sawdust.

The rest of the afternoon dragged on. Yvars felt nothing but his fatigue and his aching heart. He would have liked to talk. But he had nothing to say, nor did the others. On their taciturn faces could be read only sorrow and a kind of obstinacy. Sometimes inside him the word *misfortune* began to take shape, but just barely, and it disappeared instantly like a bubble blown and burst at the same time. He badly wanted to go home, to find Fernande, the boy, and the terrace too. Just then Ballester announced closing time. The machines stopped.

Without hurrying, they went one by one to the cloakroom. Said stayed behind, he had to clean the work spaces and water down the dusty ground. When Yvars arrived at the cloakroom, Esposito, enormous and hairy, was already taking a shower. He had his back turned toward them, while soaping himself up noisily. Usually, they teased him about his modesty; this huge bear obstinately hid his private parts. But no one seemed to notice that day. Esposito backed out and wrapped a towel around his hips like a loincloth. The others took their turns, and Marcou was vigorously clapping his naked flanks when they heard the large door roll slowly on its cast-iron wheel. Lassalle entered.

He was dressed as he had been on his first visit, but his hair was a little disheveled. He stopped on the threshold, contemplated the vast deserted workshop, stopped again, and looked toward the cloakroom. Esposito, still covered by his loincloth, turned toward him. Naked, embarrassed, he shifted from one foot to the other. Yvars thought that it was up to Marcou to say something. But Marcou kept himself invisible behind the rain of water that surrounded him. Esposito grabbed a shirt, and was pulling it on hurriedly when Lassalle said, "Goodnight," in a slightly muffled voice, and began to walk toward the back door. When Yvars thought they should have called to him, the door was already closing.

Yvars then got dressed without washing up, said goodnight himself, but with all his heart, and they answered with the same warmth. He went out quickly, found his bicycle and, when he mounted, his back pain. Now he was cycling into the last of the afternoon, through the bustling town. He was going quickly, he wanted to reach the old house and the terrace. He would wash up in the laundry room before sitting down to watch the sea that already kept him company, darker than this morning, above the ramps of the boulevard. But the little girl, too, kept him company, and he could not stop thinking about her.

At the house, the boy had come home from school and was reading the comics. Fernande asked Yvars whether everything was okay. He said nothing, washed up in the laundry room, then sat on the bench against the little wall of the terrace. The mended linen was hanging above him, the sky was growing transparent; beyond the wall, they could see the soft evening sea. Fernande brought the anisette, two glasses, the jug of fresh water. She sat down beside her husband. He told her everything, holding her hand as he had done early in their marriage. When he had finished, he sat motionless, turned toward the sea, where the swift dusk was already running from one end of the horizon to the other. "Ah, that's the trouble!" he said. He would have liked to be young again, and Fernande too, and they would have gone away, across the sea.

The Guest

The schoolteacher watched the two men climbing toward him. One was on horseback, the other on foot. They had not yet tackled the steep path that led to the school, built on the hillside. They were struggling more and more slowly in the snow, among the stones, on the vast expanse of the high desert plateau. From time to time the horse visibly stumbled. They were not yet within earshot, but he could see clearly the jet of vapor coming from the horse's nostrils. One of the men, at least, knew the country. They were following the path that had disappeared several days ago under a dirty white cover. The teacher calculated that they would not be on the hill for half an hour. He was feeling cold; he went back into the school to find a sweater.

He crossed the empty, icy classroom. On the blackboard the four rivers of France, drawn with four different colored chalks, had been running toward their estuary for three days now. The snow had fallen abruptly in mid-October, after eight months of dryness, without any rain to ease the transition, and the twenty or so students who lived in the villages scattered on the plateau had stopped coming. They would have to wait for the good weather. Daru now heated only the single room that was his lodging, which was adjacent to the classroom and also opened onto the plateau to the east. His window, too, like those of the classroom, looked toward the south. On that side, the school was situated a few kilometers from the place where the plateau began to descend southward. In clear weather one could see the purple masses of the mountain foothills that opened onto the desert.

Feeling a little warmer, Daru returned to the window from which he had first glimpsed the two men. They could no longer be seen, so they must have tackled the steep path. The sky was lighter; the snow had stopped falling during the night. Morning broke with a dirty light that became only a little brighter as the ceiling of clouds lifted. It was as if the day were just beginning at two o'clock in the afternoon. But this was better than those three days when the thick snow fell amid incessant darkness, with little gusts of wind that rattled the double doors of the classroom. Daru had patiently borne the long hours in his room, leaving it only to go to the shed and look after the chickens and take in the allotment of coal. Fortunately, the truck from Tadjid, the nearest village to the north, had brought fresh supplies two days before the blizzard. It would return in forty-eight hours.

Besides, he had what he needed to sustain a siege, the little room crowded with sacks of wheat, which the administration left him in reserve to distribute to those of his students whose families had been victims of the drought. In reality, misfortune had touched them all since all of them were poor. Every day Daru would distribute a ration to the children. They missed it, he knew, during these bad days. Perhaps one of the fathers or big brothers would come this evening and he would give them fresh supplies of grain. They had to bridge the gap to the next harvest, that's all. Now cargo ships full of wheat were arriving from France, the worst was over. But it would be difficult to forget that wretchedness, that army of ragged ghosts wandering in the sun, the plateaus charred month after month, the earth shriveling little by little, literally scorched, every stone bursting into dust underfoot. The sheep had died then by the thousands, and a few men here and there, without anyone noticing.

Before this wretchedness, Daru—living almost like a monk in his remote schoolhouse, and content even with the little he had and with this rough life—had felt like a lord, with his whitewashed walls, his narrow couch, his unfinished shelves, his well, and his weekly supplies of water and food. And suddenly this snow, without warning, without the release of rain. The country was like that, a cruel place to live, even without the men, who didn't help matters. But Daru had been born here. Anywhere else, he felt exiled.

He left and walked out on the terraced ground in front of the school. The two men were now halfway up the slope. He recognized the horseman as Balducci, the old gendarme he had known for a long time. Balducci was holding the end of a rope, leading an Arab who was following behind him, his hands tied, his head bowed. The gendarme made a gesture of greeting to which Daru did not respond, entirely occupied as he was in looking at the Arab dressed in a faded blue djellaba, his feet in sandals but covered with socks of crude oatmeal wool, wearing a short, narrow *chèche* on his head. They were approaching. Balducci held his animal at a walk so as not to hurt the Arab, and the group was advancing slowly.

Within earshot, Balducci cried: "One hour to do three kilometers from El Ameur!" Daru did not answer. Short and square in his thick sweater, he watched them climb. Not once had the Arab raised his head. "Greetings," Daru said when they reached the terraced ground. "Come in and warm up." Balducci got laboriously down from his animal, without letting go of the rope. From under his bristling mustache he smiled at the teacher. His small dark eyes, deep-set under his sunburned forehead, and his mouth surrounded by wrinkles, gave him an attentive and industrious look. Daru took the bridle, led the animal to the shed and came back to the two men, who were now waiting for him in the school. He urged them to come into his room. "I'm going to heat the classroom," he said. "We'll be more comfortable there." When he entered the room again, Balducci was on the couch. He had untied the rope that bound him to the Arab, who was squatting near the stove. His hands still tied, the *chèche* now pushed back, he was looking toward the window. Daru saw at first only his huge lips, full, smooth, almost Negroid; the nose, however, was straight, the eyes dark and feverish. The *chèche* revealed a stubborn forehead and, beneath the sunbaked skin somewhat discolored by the cold, the whole face had an anxious and rebellious look that struck Daru when the Arab, turning his face toward him, looked him straight in the eyes. "Go next door," said the teacher, "I'll make you some mint tea."

"Thanks," Balducci said. "What a chore! I can't wait to retire." And addressing his prisoner in Arabic: "Come on, you." The Arab stood up and slowly, holding his bound wrists in front of him, went into the schoolroom.

Along with the tea, Daru brought a chair. But Balducci was already ensconced at the first table, and the Arab had squatted against the teacher's platform opposite the stove, which stood between the desk and the window. When Daru held out the glass of tea to the prisoner, he hesitated at the sight of his bound hands. "Perhaps we can untie him." "Sure," Balducci said. "It was for the trip here." He was about to get up. But Daru, setting the glass on the floor, had knelt next to the Arab. Without saying anything, the man watched him with feverish eyes. Once his hands were free, he rubbed his swollen wrists against each other, took the glass of tea, and inhaled the burning liquid in small, quick sips.

"Good," Daru said. "And where are you headed?"

Balducci pulled his mustache out of the tea: "Here, son."

"Odd students! Are you sleeping here?"

"No. I'm going back to El Ameur. And you're going to turn in this comrade at Tinguit. They're expecting you at headquarters."

Balducci looked at Daru with a friendly little smile.

"What's this nonsense," the teacher said. "Are you kidding me?"

"No, son. Those are the orders."

"Orders? I'm not . . ." Daru hesitated, not wanting to insult the old Corsican. "Well, that's not my job."

"Hey, what does that mean? In wartime, people do all sorts of jobs."

"Then I'll wait for the declaration of war!"

Balducci nodded approval.

"Okay. But those are the orders and they include you, too. Things are moving, it seems. There's talk of rebellion next. In a sense, we're already mobilized."

Daru remained obstinate.

"Listen, son," Balducci said. "I'm fond of you, and you must understand. There are a dozen of us at El Ameur to patrol the territory of a small district, and I must get back. I was told to hand this guy over to you and return without delay. They couldn't keep him there. His village was in an uproar, they wanted to free him. You must take him to Tinguit during the day tomorrow. Twenty kilometers shouldn't frighten a tough guy like you. After that, it'll be over. You'll have your students again and your comfortable life."

Behind the wall, the horse could be heard snorting and

pawing the ground. Daru looked out the window. The weather was definitely improving, it was growing lighter on the snowy plateau. When all the snow melted, the sun would reign again and burn the fields of stone once more. For days, the unchanging sky would again spill its dry light over the solitary expanse where nothing spoke of man.

"So," he said, turning again toward Balducci, "what's he done?" And before the gendarme had opened his mouth, Daru asked, "Does he speak French?"

"No, not a word. We've been looking for him for a month, but they were hiding him. He killed his cousin."

"Is he against us?"

"I don't think so. But you never know."

"Why did he kill him?"

"Family business, I think. One owed the other grain, it seems. It's not clear. Anyway, he killed the cousin with a bill-hook. You know, the way you'd kill a sheep, *zip!* . . ."

Balducci made a gesture of drawing a blade across his throat, and the Arab, his attention attracted, watched him with a kind of anxiety. Daru felt a sudden anger against this man, against all men and their filthy spite, their inexhaustible hatreds, their bloodlust.

But the kettle was whistling on the stove. He served Balducci more tea, hesitated, then served the Arab again, who drank avidly for the second time. His djellaba fell half open as he raised his arms, and the teacher glimpsed his thin, muscular chest.

"Thanks, kid," Balducci said. "And now, I'm off."

He stood up and went toward the Arab, pulling a small rope out of his pocket.

"What are you doing?" Daru asked drily.

Balducci, interrupted, showed him the rope.

"Don't bother."

The old gendarme hesitated.

"As you like. You're armed of course?"

"I have my hunting rifle."

"Where?"

"In the trunk."

"You ought to have it near your bed."

"Why? I have nothing to fear."

"You're cracked, son. If they rise up, no one's protected, we're all in the same boat."

"I'll defend myself. I'll have time to see them coming."

Balducci started laughing, then suddenly the mustache covered his white teeth again.

"You have time? Okay, that's what I was saying. You've always been a little crazy. That's why I like you so much, my son was like that."

At the same time he took out his revolver and put it on the desk.

"Keep it, I don't need two weapons from here to El Ameur."

The revolver glistened on the black paint of the table. When the gendarme turned toward him, the teacher inhaled the smell of horse and leather.

"Listen, Balducci," Daru said suddenly, "all this disgusts

me, and your boy first and foremost. But I won't turn him in. Fight for myself, yes, if need be. But not that."

The old gendarme stood in front of him and looked at him severely.

"You're being stupid," he said slowly. "Me neither, I don't like it. To put a rope on a man, even after years you don't get used to it and yes, you even feel ashamed. But you can't let them get away with it."

"I won't turn him in," Daru repeated.

"It's an order, son. I repeat it to you."

"Fine. Repeat to them what I've told you: I won't turn him in."

Balducci made a visible effort at reflection. He looked at the Arab and at Daru. Finally, he made up his mind.

"No. I won't tell them anything. If you want to break with us, go ahead, I won't denounce you. I have orders to hand over the prisoner: I'm doing it. Now you're going to sign this paper for me."

"That's pointless. I won't deny you left him with me."

"Don't get nasty with me. I know that you'll tell the truth. You're from this place and you're a man. But you must sign, that's the rule."

Daru opened his drawer, took out a small square bottle of purple ink, the red wooden penholder with the *sergeant-major* pen he used to trace penmanship models, and he signed. The gendarme carefully folded the paper and put it in his wallet. Then he headed toward the door.

"I'll walk you out," Daru said.

75

"No," said Balducci. "It's no good being polite. You've insulted me."

He looked at the Arab, still in the same place, smiled ruefully, and turned back toward the door: "Farewell, son," he said. The door banged behind him. Balducci appeared outside the window, then disappeared. His footsteps were muffled by the snow. Behind the partition, the horse stirred excitedly, the chickens flapped about in alarm. A moment later, Balducci passed in front of the window again, leading the horse by the bridle. He advanced toward the steep path without looking back and disappeared first, the horse following. They heard a big stone rolling softly. Daru came back to the prisoner, who, without moving, had not taken his eyes off him. "Wait," the teacher said in Arabic, and he headed toward his room. As he crossed the threshold, he changed his mind, went to the desk, took the revolver and stuck it in his pocket. Then, without turning around, he went into his room.

For a long time he lay on his couch watching the sky gradually close over, listening to the silence. It was this silence that had seemed difficult to him in the first days of his arrival, after the war. He had requested a post in a small town at the base of the foothills that separate the high plateaus from the desert. There, rocky walls, green and black to the north, pink or mauve to the south, marked the frontier of eternal summer. He had been assigned a post farther to the north, on the plateau itself. In the beginning, the solitude and silence had been hard for him in these merciless lands inhabited only by stones. Sometimes the furrows seemed agricultural, but they had been dug to find a certain kind of stone useful in construction. The only labor here was harvesting pebbles. Otherwise, people scratched a few shavings of earth accumulated in the hollows to enrich the meager village gardens. This is how it was, stones alone covered three-quarters of this country. Towns sprang up here, flourished, then disappeared; men passed through, loved each other or cut each other's throats, then died. In this desert, no one, neither he nor his guest, mattered. And yet outside this desert, neither of them, Daru knew, could have truly lived.

When he got up, no sound was coming from the classroom. He was astonished at the surge of joy he felt at the mere thought that the Arab might have escaped and that he would find himself once more alone with no decision to make. But the prisoner was there. He had simply stretched out on the floor between the stove and the desk. His eyes were open, he was staring at the ceiling. In this position, his thick lips were most noticeable, as though he were pouting. "Come," Daru said. The Arab got up and followed him. In the bedroom, the teacher showed him a chair near the table, under the window. The Arab sat down without taking his eyes off Daru.

"Are you hungry?"

"Yes," said the prisoner.

Daru set two places. He took flour and oil, kneaded a flat cake in a pan, and lit the little stove with butane. While the flat cake was cooking, he went out to the shed to gather cheese, eggs, dates, and condensed milk. When the flat cake was done, he put it to cool on the windowsill, heated up the condensed milk diluted with water, and to finish, beat the eggs into an omelet. In one of his movements, he knocked the revolver stuffed into his right pocket. He set the bowl down, went into the classroom, and put the revolver in his desk drawer. When he came back into the room, night was falling. He put on the light and served the Arab: "Eat," he said. The other took a piece of the flat cake, brought it quickly to his mouth, and stopped.

"And you?" he said.

"After you. I'll eat, too."

The thick lips opened a little, the Arab hesitated, then bit resolutely into the flat cake.

With the meal finished, the Arab looked at the teacher.

"Are you the judge?"

"No, I'm keeping you until tomorrow."

"Why are you eating with me?"

"I'm hungry."

The other fell silent. Daru got up and went out. He brought back a camp bed from the shed, opened it between the table and the stove, perpendicular to his own. From a large trunk that stood in a corner and served as a file shelf, he pulled out two blankets, which he arranged on the camp bed. Then he stopped, felt useless, and sat down on his own bed. There was no more to do or prepare. He had to take a look at this man. And so he looked at him, trying to imagine this face transported by rage. He couldn't manage it. He saw nothing but the dark, shining eyes, and the animal mouth.

"Why did you kill him?" he said in a voice whose hostility surprised him.

The Arab turned away from his gaze.

"He was running away. I ran after him."

He raised his eyes to Daru, and they were full of a sort of unhappy questioning.

"What will they do to me now?"

"Are you afraid?"

The other stiffened, shifting his eyes away.

"Are you sorry?"

The Arab stared at him, his mouth open. Clearly, he did not understand Daru. At the same time he was feeling clumsy and awkward with his big body squeezed between two beds.

"Lie down there," Daru said impatiently. "It's your bed."

The Arab did not move. He appealed to Daru:

"Tell me!"

The teacher looked at him.

"Will the gendarme come back tomorrow?"

"I don't know."

"Are you coming with us?"

"I don't know. Why?"

The prisoner got up and stretched out on top of the blankets, his feet toward the window. The light from the electric bulb fell straight into his eyes, which he closed at once.

"Why?" Daru repeated, standing in front of the bed.

The Arab opened his eyes under the blinding light and looked at him, forcing himself not to blink.

"Come with us," he said.

In the middle of the night, Daru was not asleep. He had gone to bed after undressing completely—he usually slept naked. But when he realized he was in bed with nothing on, he hesitated. He felt vulnerable and was tempted to get dressed again. Then he shrugged his shoulders. He had seen others like that, and if need be he would break his adversary in two. From his bed he could observe him, stretched out on his back, motionless as ever, his eyes closed under the violent light. When Daru put the light out, the shadows seemed to congeal at once. Again the night came alive outside the window, where the starless sky gently shifted. The teacher soon distinguished the body stretched out in front of him. The Arab never moved, but his eyes seemed open. A light wind prowled around the school. Perhaps it would chase the clouds away and the sun would return.

In the night the wind increased. The chickens became agitated, then quieted down. The Arab turned on his side, with his back to Daru, who thought he heard him moan. He waited for his breathing to become stronger and more regular. He listened to this breath so near and daydreamed without being able to sleep. In the room where he had slept alone for a year, this presence disturbed him. But it disturbed him also by imposing on him a sort of brotherhood, which he rejected in the present circumstances, familiar as it was. Men who share the same sleeping quarters, soldiers and prisoners, develop a strange bond, as if shedding their weapons with their clothes, they were joined together each evening, beyond their differences, in the ancient community of dreams and fatigue. But Daru shook himself, he did not like this nonsense, he needed to sleep.

A little later, however, when the Arab stirred imperceptibly, the teacher was still not asleep. When the prisoner moved a second time, Daru stiffened, on the alert. The Arab raised himself slowly on his arms, with an almost somnambulistic movement. Sitting in the bed, he waited, motionless, without turning his head toward Daru, as if he were listening attentively. Daru did not move. It occurred to him that the revolver was still in his desk drawer. It would be better to act at once. He continued to observe the prisoner, however, who with the same smooth movement placed his feet on the ground, waited again, then began to stand up slowly. Daru was about to interrupt him when the Arab began to walk, this time quite naturally but with extraordinary silence. He was heading toward the door at the back that led to the shed. He lifted the latch cautiously and went out, pushing the door closed behind him without shutting it. Daru had not moved. "He's running away," he thought. "Good riddance!" Still, he listened with keen attention. The chickens were not stirring; therefore the other man was on the plateau. A faint sound of water came to him, which he understood only when the Arab was framed in the doorway again, carefully shut the door, and lay down once more without a sound. Then Daru turned his back to him and slept. Still later, from the depths of his sleep, he seemed to hear furtive steps outside the schoolhouse. "I'm dreaming, I'm dreaming!" he repeated to himself. And he slept on.

When he woke, the sky was clear; the poorly installed window let in a cold, pure air. The Arab was sleeping, now huddled under the blankets, his mouth open, in complete abandon. But when Daru shook him, he started in terror, looking at Daru without recognizing him, his eyes wild and such a frightened expression on his face that the teacher took a step back. "Don't be afraid. It's me. Time to eat." The Arab shook his head and said yes. Calm had returned to his face, but his expression was absent and distracted.

The coffee was ready. They drank it, both of them sitting on the camp bed, chewing their pieces of flat cake. Then Daru led the Arab under the shed and showed him the faucet where he washed up. He came back into the room, folded the covers and the camp bed, made his own bed, and tidied up the room. Then he passed through the schoolroom and went out onto the terraced ground in front of the building. The sun was already rising in the blue sky; a bright and gentle light was flooding the desert plateau. On the steep path the snow was melting in places. The stones would appear again. Crouched on the edge of the plateau, the teacher contemplated the deserted expanse. He was thinking of Balducci. He had insulted him, he'd sent him off, in a way, as if he did not want to be in the same boat. He could still hear the gendarme's farewell, and without knowing why, he felt strangely empty and vulnerable. At that moment, from the other side of the school, the prisoner coughed. Daru listened to him, in spite of himself, then, furious, threw a pebble that whistled in the air before landing in the snow. The idiotic crime and the man himself revolted him, but to turn him in was dishonorable; just thinking about it filled him with humiliation. And he cursed both his own people, who had sent him this Arab, and the man himself who had dared to kill and hadn't known enough to run away. Daru stood up, took a turn around the terraced ground, waited, motionless, then went into the school.

The Arab, leaning over the cement floor of the shed, was washing his teeth with two fingers. Daru looked at him.

"Come," he said.

He went back into the bedroom ahead of the prisoner. He slipped on a hunting jacket over his sweater and pulled on his walking shoes. He stood waiting until the Arab had put on his *chèche* and his sandals. They went through the schoolroom, and the teacher showed his companion the way out. "Go on," he said. The other did not move. "I'm coming," Daru said. The Arab went out. Daru went back to the room and made a packet with biscuits, dates, and sugar. In the classroom, before leaving, he hesitated a moment in front of his desk, then he crossed the threshold of the school and locked the door. "It's that way," he said. He took the path going east, followed by the prisoner. But not far from the school, he thought he heard a slight noise behind him. He retraced his steps, inspected the surroundings of the building; no one was there. The Arab watched him without seeming to understand. "Let's go," Daru said.

They walked for an hour and rested near a kind of limestone needle. The snow was melting faster and faster, the sun was quickly swallowing up the puddles, furiously cleaning the plateau, which gradually dried out and vibrated like the air itself. When they set off on their way again, the ground echoed beneath their feet. Here and there a bird sliced the space in front of them with a joyous cry. Daru took deep breaths of the fresh light. A kind of exaltation rose in him before the vast familiar space, almost entirely yellow now under its cap of blue sky. They walked another hour, descending toward the south. They reached a kind of flat perch, made of crumbling rocks. From there the plateau hurtled down to the east, toward a low plain where they could distinguish a few sparse trees and, to the south, toward the rocky outcroppings that gave the landscape a tormented aspect.

Daru surveyed the two directions. There was nothing but sky on the horizon, not a man to be seen. He turned toward the Arab, who was looking at him uncomprehendingly. Daru held out the packet to him: "Take it," he said. "It's dates, bread, and sugar. You can hold out for two days. Here are a thousand francs, too." The Arab took the packet and the money, but he kept his full hands at chest level, as if he did not know what to do with what he had been given. "Now look," said the teacher, and he pointed to the east "that's the way to Tinguit. You've got a two-hour walk. In Tinguit, there's the administration and the police. They're expecting you." The Arab was looking toward the east, still holding the packet and the money against his chest. Daru took his arm and turned him, a little roughly, toward the south. Below the peak where they stood, they could make out a faint path. "There, that's the trail across the plateau. A day's walk from here you'll find pastures and the first nomads. They will welcome you and give you shelter, according to their law." The Arab turned back around now toward Daru, and a sort of panic appeared on his face. "Listen," he said. Daru shook his head: "No, be quiet. Now I'm leaving you." He turned his back and took two big steps in the direction of the school, looked indecisively at the motionless Arab, and started off again. For a few minutes he heard only his own steps echoing on the cold earth, and he did not turn his head. A moment later, however, he turned around. The Arab was still there, at the edge of the hill, his arms hanging now, and he was looking at the teacher. Daru felt a lump in his throat. But he cursed impatiently, made a sweeping gesture, and set off again. He was already at some distance when he stopped again and looked. There was no one on the hill.

Daru hesitated. The sun was now rather high in the sky and beginning to burn his forehead. The teacher retraced his steps, at first uncertainly, then with decision. When he reached the little hill, he was streaming with sweat. He tackled it at top speed and stopped, out of breath, at the top. The fields of rock to the south stood clearly etched on the blue sky, but on the plain, to the east, the vapor was already rising. And in this light haze, Daru, his heart aching, discovered the Arab slowly making his way along the road to the prison.

A little later, standing in front of the classroom window, the teacher watched distractedly as the yellow light leaped from the heights of the sky and spread across the whole surface of

the plateau. Behind him, on the blackboard, among the me-
anderings of the French rivers, a clumsy hand had traced in
chalk the inscription he had just read: "You turned in our
brother. You will pay." Daru was looking at the sky, the plateau,
and beyond at the invisible lands that reached all the way to
the sea. In this vast country he had loved so much, he was
alone.

Jonas,

or The Artist at Work

Cast me into the sea . . .
For I know that for my sake
This great tempest is upon you.

JONAH 1:12

Gilbert Jonas, artist and painter, believed in his star. Indeed, it was all he believed in, although he felt respect and even a kind of admiration for the religion of others. His own faith, however, had its virtues, since it consisted of admitting, somehow obscurely, that he had done nothing to merit what he had achieved. And when, around his thirty-fifth year, a dozen critics suddenly fought over the glory of discovering his talent, he showed not the slightest surprise. But his serenity, attributed by some to smugness, could on the contrary be entirely explained by a trusting modesty. Jonas gave credit to his star rather than his merits.

He showed rather more surprise when an art dealer offered him a monthly stipend that freed him from all cares. The architect Rateau, who had loved Jonas and his star since their school days, argued with him in vain that this monthly

87

stipend was hardly a decent living, and that the art dealer had nothing to lose. "All the same," Jonas said. Rateau, who succeeded in everything he did by sheer hard work, goaded his friend. "What's this 'all the same'? You can negotiate." This was useless. Deep down, Jonas thanked his star. "As you like," he told the art dealer. And he gave up his position in the family publishing house to devote himself entirely to painting. "What luck!" he said.

In reality he was thinking: "My luck goes on." As far back as he could remember, he found this luck at work. He felt a fond gratitude toward his parents, first because they had raised him distractedly, which allowed him the leisure to daydream, then because they had separated on grounds of adultery. At least that was the pretext claimed by his father, who forgot to specify that it was a rather peculiar sort of adultery: he could not stand his wife's good works. She was well nigh a secular saint who saw no malice in making a gift of herself to suffering humanity. But the husband insisted on being master of his wife's virtues. "I've had enough," this Othello said, "of being cuckolded by the poor."

This misunderstanding was to Jonas's advantage. Having read or heard of several sadistic murderers who were the offspring of divorce, his parents vied to lavish him with treats and nip in the bud any such distressing development. Less apparent were the effects of the shock, according to them, to the child's consciousness, and so they worried even more, for invisible damage must be deepest. If Jonas announced that he was happy with himself or his day, his parents' usual anxiety verged on panic. Their attentions redoubled and the child then wanted for nothing.

His presumed misfortune finally earned Jonas a devoted brother in the person of his friend Rateau. Rateau's parents often invited his little school friend, pleading his unhappiness. Their pitying remarks inspired in their son, a vigorous sportsman, a desire to take under his protection the child whose effortless success he already admired. Admiration and condescension made a good mix in a friendship that Jonas received, like everything else, with encouraging simplicity.

When Jonas had completed his studies—without any special effort—he again had the luck to join his father's publishing house, finding a position there and, indirectly, his vocation as painter. As the most prestigious publisher in France, Jonas's father was of the opinion that more than ever, and indeed owing to the cultural crisis, the book was the future. "History shows," he would say, "that the less people read the more they buy books." A trendsetter himself, he only rarely read the manuscripts submitted to him, decided to publish strictly on the basis of the author's personality or the timeliness of his subject (since in this view sex was the only ever-timely subject, the publisher eventually specialized), and was strictly interested in finding novelties and free publicity. Along with the manuscript department, then, Jonas took over a lot of spare time. That was how he came to painting.

For the first time he discovered an unexpected and inexhaustible passion, soon devoted his days to painting, and—always effortlessly—excelled in that practice. Nothing else seemed to interest him, and it was unlikely that he would marry at a reasonable age, as painting entirely consumed him. For the beings and ordinary circumstances of life he had only a benevolent smile, which exempted him from concerning himself further. It took a motorcycle accident—Rateau was driving too fast, with his friend riding behind—for Jonas, his right hand immobilized in a cast, and feeling bored, to become interested in love. Here again he was inclined to see the good effects of his star in this serious accident. Without it, he would not have taken the time to notice Louise Poulin as she deserved.

According to Rateau, moreover, Louise did not deserve to be noticed. Short and stocky himself, he liked only tall women. "I don't know what you see in that little ant," he said. Louise was in fact petite, with dark complexion, hair, and eyes, but she had a nice shape and a pretty face. Jonas, tall and solid, felt tenderly toward the ant, especially because she was industrious. Louise's vocation was activity. Such a vocation happily complemented Jonas's taste for inertia, and for its advantages. Louise devoted herself first to literature, at least as long as she believed that publishing interested Jonas. She read everything indiscriminately, and in a matter of weeks became capable of talking about it all. Jonas admired her and decided that he was definitely exempt from reading since Louise kept him sufficiently informed and up-to-date on the basics of contemporary discoveries. "You mustn't say," Louise announced, "that someone is bad or ugly but that he chooses to be bad or ugly." The distinction was important and might well lead, at the very least, as Rateau pointed out, to the condemnation of the human race. But Louise settled the matter by pointing out that since this truth was supported by both the tabloid press and philosophical reviews, it was therefore universal and beyond dispute. "As you like," said Jonas, who immediately forgot this cruel discovery to dream on his star.

Louise deserted literature when she realized that Jonas was only interested in painting. She immediately devoted herself to the plastic arts, ran to museums and exhibitions, and dragged Jonas along, although he could hardly understand the painting of his contemporaries and in his artistic simplicity found it troubling. Yet he rejoiced at being so well informed on everything that concerned his art. It is true that the next day he would forget the name of the painter whose works he had just seen. But Louise was right when she peremptorily reminded him of one of the certainties she had preserved from her literary period, the knowledge that in reality, nothing is ever forgotten. His star certainly protected Jonas, who could in this way guiltlessly accumulate the certainties of memory and the conveniences of forgetting.

But the treasures of devotion Louise lavished upon him sparkled brightest in Jonas's daily life. This good angel spared him the purchases of shoes, clothing, and underwear that for any normal man shorten the days of an already brief life. She resolutely took charge of the thousand inventions of the time-killing machine, from the obscure paperwork involved in social security to endlessly multiplying fiscal arrangements. "Yes, okay," Rateau would say, "but she can't go to the dentist for you." She did not do that, but she telephoned and made appointments at the best times; she took care of oil changes for the car, hotel rentals for vacations, domestic heating; she bought whatever gifts Jonas wanted to give, chose and sent his flowers, and still found time on certain evenings to come by his place in his absence and make up the bed that he would not need to turn down that night before going to sleep.

With the same spirit, naturally, she got into this bed, then made the appointment at City Hall, led Jonas there two years before his talent was finally recognized, and organized the honeymoon so that they could visit all the museums. Not without first managing to find, in the midst of a housing crisis, a three-room apartment where they settled on their return. She then produced two children in quick succession, a boy and a girl, in accordance with her plan to have a total of three, which she completed shortly after Jonas had left the publishing house to devote himself to painting.

Once she had given birth, however, Louise devoted herself entirely to her child, then to her children. She still tried to help her husband, but she had no time. To be sure, she regretted neglecting Jonas, but her decisive character prevented her from lingering on these regrets. "Oh well," she often said, "to each his own workbench." An expression that seemed to delight Jonas, for like all the artists of his time, he wanted to be considered an artisan. So the artisan was a little neglected and had to buy his shoes himself. However, apart from the fact that this was in the nature of things, Jonas was tempted to congratulate himself. Certainly he had to make the effort to visit the shops, but this effort was rewarded by one of those hours of solitude that only enhances a couple's happiness.

The problem of usable space, however, prevailed over other household problems, for time and space were shrinking around them at the same rate. The birth of the children, Jonas's new profession, their cramped digs, and the modest stipend that ruled out the purchase of a larger apartment left only a narrow field for Louise and Jonas's respective activities. The apartment was on the second floor of what had been, in the eighteenth century, a private townhouse in an old quarter of the capital. Many artists lived in this part of the city, faithful to the principle that in art, the search for the new must be done within a framework of the old. Jonas, who shared this conviction, was delighted to be living in this quarter.

For old his apartment certainly was. But some very modern arrangements had given it an original character that consisted chiefly of offering its residents a great volume of air while occupying only a limited surface. The rooms, unusually high and graced with magnificent windows, had surely been intended—to judge by their majestic proportions—for grand receptions and ceremonial dress. But the necessities of urban crowding and real-estate profits had forced successive landlords to divide these vast rooms with partitions and so to multiply the stalls, which they rented at top dollar to their herd of tenants. They set particular value on what they called "the important square footage of air." The advantage was undeniable. This could only be attributed to the impossibility of partitioning the rooms' vertical space as well. Even so, the landlords did not hesitate to make the necessary sacrifices to offer some additional refuge to the upcoming generation, especially to the married and multiplying of that era. Besides, the square footage of air offered not only advantages; it offered the inconvenience of making the rooms difficult to heat in winter, and this unfortunately obliged the landlords to increase the heating bill. In summer, due to the vast glass surfaces, the apartment was literally violated by light: there were no blinds. The landlords had neglected to install them, no doubt discouraged by the height of the windows and the cost of carpentry. After all, thick curtains could perform the same function, and posed no problem as to cost since they were charged to the tenants. The landlords certainly did not refuse to help and provided curtains from their own stores at unbeatable prices. Indeed, philanthropic real estate was their hobby. In their ordinary lives these new princes sold percale and velvet.

Jonas was ecstatic at the apartment's advantages and had no trouble accepting its drawbacks. "As you like," he said to the landlord about the heating bill. As for the curtains, he agreed with Louise that it was enough to provide them for the only bedroom and leave the other windows bare. "We have nothing to hide," said that pure heart. Jonas had been especially charmed by the largest room, whose ceiling was so high that any lighting installation was out of the question. This room was entered directly from the outside, and connected by a narrow hallway to the two much smaller ones lined up behind it. At the end of the apartment was the kitchen, next to the

WC, and a cubbyhole graced with the name of shower room. It could indeed pass as such, providing they installed the fixture vertically and were willing to stand absolutely still to receive its beneficial spray.

The truly extraordinary height of the ceilings and the cramped nature of the rooms made this apartment an odd assemblage of almost entirely glassed-in parallelepipeds, all doors and windows, where furniture could find no supporting wall and human beings, lost in the white and violent light, seemed to float like bottled imps in a vertical aquarium. Furthermore, all the windows looked out onto the courtyard and—from scarcely any distance—onto other windows of the same style, behind which could be glimpsed the stately outline of new windows opening onto a second courtyard. "It's a hall of mirrors," said Jonas, thrilled. On Rateau's advice, they decided to place the marriage bed in one of the small rooms, the other being necessary to shelter the child that was already on its way. The large room served as Jonas's studio during the day, as living room in the evening and at mealtimes. Besides, they could eat in the kitchen if necessary, provided that Jonas or Louise was willing to stand. Rateau, for his part, had installed any number of ingenious devices. With sliding doors, retractable shelves, and folding tables, he had managed to compensate for the scarcity of furniture by accentuating this original apartment's resemblance to a set of Chinese boxes.

But when the rooms were full of pictures and children, they needed to think quickly about a new arrangement. Before the birth of their third child, Jonas worked in the large room, Louise knitted in their bedroom, while the two children occupied the last room, romping around in there, then tumbling freely through the rest of the apartment. So they decided to settle the newborn in a corner of the studio, which Jonas enclosed by making a screen of his canvases. This offered the advantage of having the baby within earshot so they could respond more readily to his cries. Besides, Jonas need never be disturbed, Louise told him. She would come into the studio before the baby cried, although with a thousand precautions and always on tiptoe. Jonas, touched by such discretion, one day assured Louise that he was not so sensitive, and that he could work quite well to the sound of her steps. Louise replied that she was also trying not to waken the baby. Full of admiration for her tender maternal instinct, Jonas laughed good-naturedly at his mistake. As a result, he dared not admit that Louise's prudent interventions were more disruptive than if she were to burst in openly. First because they lasted longer, then because they were done in pantomime: Louise, with her arms opened wide, her torso leaning back a little and her leg thrown up high in front of her, could hardly go unnoticed. This method even went counter to her avowed intentions, since at any moment Louise was liable to snag one of the canvases that filled the studio. Then the noise woke the baby, who expressed his discontent according to his own powerful means. The father, enchanted by his son's pulmonary capacity, would run to comfort him, then be immediately relieved by his wife. Jonas once again set up his canvases, then, brushes in hand, listened, charmed, to his son's insistent and sovereign voice.

This was about the time that Jonas's success earned him many friends. These friends materialized on the telephone or in unannounced visits. The telephone, which after due consideration had been placed in the studio, rang often, always to the detriment of the sleeping baby, who mingled his cries with the gadget's imperative ring. If Louise happened to be looking after the other children, she was forced to come running with one of them in tow, but most of the time she found Jonas holding the baby with one hand and with the other his paintbrushes and the telephone receiver, which would be transmitting a friendly invitation to lunch. Jonas was amazed that anyone would really want to have lunch with him, as his conversation was banal, but to keep his workday unbroken he preferred evening outings. Most of the time, unfortunately, the friend was free only for lunch, and for lunch that very day; he was reserving it for dear Jonas. Dear Jonas would accept: "As you like!" hang up and say: "What a good fellow!" and pass the baby to Louise. He would take up his work again, soon interrupted by lunch or dinner. Now he had to move his canvases out of the way, unfold the modified table, and sit down with the children. During the meal, Jonas would keep one eye on the painting in progress, and in the beginning at least, he found his children a little slow in chewing and swallowing, so that every meal seemed excessively drawn out. But he read in the paper that it was important to eat slowly in order to digest properly, and from then on found each meal an occasion to enjoy himself at length.

At other times his new friends would visit him. Rateau

himself came only after dinner. He was at his office during the day, and besides, he knew that painters work during daylight. But Jonas's new friends almost all belonged to the species of artists or critics. Some had painted, others were going to paint, and the critics were busy with what had been or would be painted. All of them, of course, held artistic efforts in high esteem, and complained of the organization of the modern world that makes it so difficult to pursue those very efforts and the practice of meditation so indispensable to the artist. They complained through long afternoons, begging Jonas to continue working as if they were not there, and to treat them freely, after all, they weren't philistines and knew what an artist's time was worth. Jonas, content to have made friends capable of allowing him to work in their presence, would return to his painting but continue to answer their questions or laugh at their anecdotes.

Such simplicity put his friends more and more at ease. Their good humor was so authentic that they forgot it was mealtime. The children, however, had better memories. They would rush about, mingle with the guests, shout, be taken in hand by the visitors, and bounced from knee to knee. At last the light would fade on the square of sky outlined by the courtyard, and Jonas would set down his paintbrushes. Naturally they had to invite the friends to take potluck and to go on talking late into the night, about art of course, but especially about painters without talent, plagiarists, or self-promoters, who were not there. Jonas himself liked to rise early to take advantage of the first hours of daylight. He knew that this would be difficult, that breakfast would not be ready on time, and that he himself would be tired. But he was also delighted to learn so many things in one evening that could not fail to be advantageous to him, in some invisible way, in his art. "In art, as in nature, nothing is lost," he would say. "Because of the star."

Sometimes the friends were joined by disciples: Jonas was now attracting a school. At first he had been surprised, not seeing what anyone could learn from him, since he still had everything to discover himself. The artist in him was groping in the dark; how could he teach the true paths? But he quickly understood that a disciple was not necessarily someone who aspired to learn something. More often, on the contrary, a person became a disciple for the disinterested pleasure of teaching his master. After that, Jonas could accept this surplus in honors with humility. The disciples explained to Jonas at length what he had painted, and why. Jonas thus discovered in his work many intentions that rather surprised him, and a host of things he had not put there. He thought he was poor and, thanks to his students, suddenly found he was rich. Sometimes, faced with such hitherto unknown riches, Jonas would feel a surge of pride. "It's true, though," he would say to himself. "That face in the background really does stand out. I don't honestly understand what they mean by indirect humanization. Yet I've gone rather far with that technique." But very soon he would shift this uncomfortable mastery to his star. "It's the star," he would say to himself, "that's going far. As for me, I'm staying close to Louise and the children."

The disciples, moreover, had another advantage: they forced Jonas to be stricter with himself. They ranked him so high in their conversation, particularly with regard to his conscience and his energy for work, that from now on no weakness was permissible. So he lost his old habit of nibbling on a piece of sugar or chocolate when he had finished a difficult passage, before getting back to work. Had he been alone, he might have secretly surrendered to this weakness. But he was aided in his moral progress by the nearly constant presence of his disciples and friends, with whom he would have been embarrassed to nibble some chocolate, and anyway, he could hardly interrupt the interesting conversation for such a trivial habit.

In addition, his disciples demanded that he remain faithful to his aesthetic. Jonas, who struggled long and hard to receive a moment of fleeting clarity now and then in which reality would suddenly appear in a fresh light, had only a vague idea of his own aesthetic. His disciples, on the other hand, had many contradictory and categorical ideas about it; and they were not joking. Jonas would sometimes have liked to invoke caprice, the artist's humble friend. But his disciples' frowns at certain canvases that departed from their idea forced him to reflect a little more on his art, which was all to the good.

Finally, the disciples helped Jonas in another way by obliging him to offer his opinion on their own production. Indeed, not a day passed without someone bringing him some barely sketched-in canvas that its author would place between Jonas and his painting in progress, in order to take advantage of the best light. An opinion was required. Until this period, Jonas was always secretly ashamed of his utter inability to judge a work of art. Exception was made for a handful of paintings that transported him, and for obviously crude scribblings, all of which seemed to him equally interesting and indifferent. Consequently, he was forced to provide himself with an arsenal of judgments, and varied ones at that, because his disciples, like all the artists of the capital, had a certain talent, and when they were around, it was up to him to draw adequate distinctions to satisfy each of them. This happy obligation required him, then, to forge a vocabulary and opinions on his art. Yet his natural kindness was not soured by this effort. He quickly realized that his disciples were not asking him for criticism, for which they had no use, but only encouragement and, if possible, praise. Only the praise had to be different for each. Jonas was no longer content with being his usual amiable self. He was amiable with ingenuity.

So time went by as Jonas painted amidst friends and students settled on chairs, now arranged in concentric circles around the easel. Often neighbors would appear at the windows across the way and this would add to his public. He would discuss, exchange views, examine the paintings submitted to him, smile at Louise's comings and goings, soothe the children, and warmly answer telephone calls, without ever setting down his paintbrushes, with which he would add a touch now and then to the painting he had begun. In a sense, his life was very full, all his hours were occupied, and he gave thanks to the fate that spared him from boredom. In another sense, it took many brushstrokes to fill a painting, and he sometimes thought the good thing about boredom was that it could be avoided by unremitting work. Jonas's production, though, slowed down as his friends became more interesting. Even in the rare hours when he was by himself, he felt too tired to redouble his efforts. And in these hours he could only dream of a new arrangement that would reconcile the pleasures of friendship with the advantages of boredom.

He broached the subject with Louise, who was already worrying about the two older children outgrowing their cramped room. She proposed setting them up in the large room by screening off their beds, and moving the baby into the small room where the telephone would not wake him up. Since the baby took up no space to speak of, Jonas could turn the small room into his studio. The large one would then be used for daytime visitors, and Jonas could come and go, joining his friends or working, certain that his need for isolation would be understood. Moreover, the need to put the older children to bed would allow them to cut the evenings short. "Wonderful," said Jonas, after some reflection. "And then," said Louise, "if your friends leave early, we'll see a little more of each other . . ." Jonas looked at her. A shadow of sadness passed over Louise's face. Touched, he held her and kissed her tenderly. She surrendered to him, and for a moment they were as happy as they had been at the beginning of their marriage. But she pulled herself away: perhaps the room was too small for Jonas. Louise grabbed a tape measure and they discovered that because of the crowding created by his canvases and his students', which were by far the most numerous, he was working anyway in a space that was scarcely bigger than the new one would be. Jonas began to move at once.

As luck would have it, the less he worked the greater his reputation grew. Every exhibition was anticipated and celebrated in advance. True, a small number of critics, among them two of the usual visitors to the studio, tempered the warmth of their reviews with a few reservations. But the disciples' indignation more than compensated for this small misfortune. To be sure, the disciples would assert, they prized the canvases from the first period above all, but the current explorations were laying the groundwork for a real revolution. Jonas reproached himself for the slight irritation he felt whenever they exalted his early works and thanked them effusively. Only Rateau grumbled: "Weird characters . . . They want you to stand still, like a statue . . . you're not allowed to live!" But Jonas defended his disciples: "You can't understand," he said to Rateau, "you . . . you like everything I do." Rateau laughed: "Damn it. It's not your pictures I like. It's your painting."

The pictures continued to please in any event, and after one enthusiastically received exhibition, the dealer voluntarily proposed to increase the monthly stipend. Jonas accepted, protesting his gratitude. "Listening to you," said the dealer, "anyone would think you actually care about money." Such good nature won the painter's heart. However, when he asked the dealer for permission to donate a canvas to be sold for charity, the man was anxious to know if it was a charity "that would pay." Jonas did not know. The dealer then proposed that they respect the terms of the contract, which accorded him exclusive sales rights. "A contract is a contract," he said. In theirs, no clause was found to cover charity. "As you like," said the painter.

The new household arrangement gave Jonas nothing but satisfaction. He could, in fact, isolate himself often enough to answer the numerous letters he now received, which he was too courteous to leave unanswered. Some concerned Jonas's art, others, the majority, concerned the correspondent, who wanted either to be encouraged in his vocation as painter or to ask for advice or financial aid. And the more Jonas's name appeared in the papers, the more he was solicited, like everyone else, to intervene and denounce grievous injustices. Jonas would answer, write about art, thank people, give his advice, forgo a new tie to send a little aid, and sign the high-minded protests submitted to him. "You're in politics now? Leave that to the writers and to unattractive spinsters," said Rateau. No, he signed only protests that claimed to be nonpartisan. But everyone claimed this worthy independence. For weeks at a time Jonas would drag around, his pockets sagging with correspondence constantly neglected and renewed. He would answer the most urgent, which generally came from strangers, and kept for a better moment those that demanded a lengthier reply, namely letters from friends. So many obligations in any case prohibited idle strolling and a light heart. He always felt behind and always guilty, even when he was working, which still happened now and then.

Louise was more and more taken up with the children, and exhausted herself doing everything that in other circumstances he had been able to do in the house. This made Jonas unhappy. After all, he was working for his own pleasure, whereas she was getting the worst of it. He noticed it clearly when she was out shopping. "The telephone!" the eldest would call, and Jonas would set down his picture only to return to it, his heart at peace, with an additional invitation. "Here to read the meter!" the gas man would yell at the door a child had opened for him. "Coming! Coming!" When Jonas would leave the telephone or the door, a friend, a disciple, perhaps both, would follow him into the small room to finish the conversation they had begun. Gradually, they all became familiar with the hallway, where they congregated, gossiping among themselves, calling for Jonas to take sides from a distance, even bursting briefly into the small room. "Here, at least," those who entered exclaimed, "we can see you a little, at leisure." Jonas softened: "It's true," he said. "We hardly see each other anymore." He also felt that he was disappointing those he did not see, and this saddened him. Often these were friends he would have preferred to meet. But he had no time, he could not be everywhere at once.

His reputation suffered. "He's gotten proud," people said, "since his success. He doesn't see anyone anymore." Or: "He cares only for himself." No, he loved his painting, and Louise, his children, Rateau, a few others as well, and he had sympathy for everyone. But life is short, time goes by quickly, and his own energy had its limits. It was difficult to paint the world and men and to live with them at the same time. On the other hand, he could neither complain nor explain his difficulties. Because then someone would slap him on the back: "Lucky bastard! That's the price of fame!"

So the mail accumulated, the disciples would not allow any relaxation, and now society people flocked to him. Jonas thought they were interested in painting when, like everyone else, they might have been equally fascinated by the English royal family or gourmet restaurants. In truth, they were society women in particular, but their manners had great simplicity. They did not buy any pictures themselves and brought their friends to the artist only in the hope, which was often disappointed, that the friends would buy instead. On the other hand, these ladies helped Louise, especially by serving tea to the visitors. The cups passed from hand to hand, traveled down the hallway from the kitchen to the large room, coming around again to rest in the small studio where Jonas, amidst a handful of friends and visitors who filled the room, continued to paint until he had to set down his paintbrushes to accept, with gratitude, the cup that a fascinating lady had filled specially for him.

He would drink his tea, look at the sketch that a disciple had just placed on his easel, laugh with his friends, interrupt himself to ask one of them to be so good as to post the packet of letters he had written the night before, set his second child back on her feet, pose for a photograph, and then: "Jonas, the telephone!" He would brandish his cup, push his way apologetically through the crowd in the hall, return, paint in a corner of the picture, stop to answer the fascinating lady that yes, certainly he would do her portrait, and return to the easel. He was working, but: "Jonas, a signature!"—"What is it now?" he said, "The mailman?"—"No, the convicts in Kashmir."—"I'm coming, I'm coming!" Then he would run to the door to receive a young friend of humanity and his letter of protest, anxiously inquire if it was a political matter, sign after receiving complete assurance along with remonstrations on the duties of his privileged life as an artist, and reappear so that someone might introduce him to a new boxing champion or the greatest playwright from a foreign country, though he could not make out the name. The playwright would stand there for five minutes, expressing with emotional eye contact what his ignorance of French prevented him from saying more clearly, while Jonas would nod his head with sincere sympathy. Happily, this insoluble situation would be interrupted by the sudden entrance of the latest charmer who wanted to be introduced to the great painter. Jonas, so delighted to make his acquaintance, would say that was him, tap the letters in his pocket, grab his paintbrushes, and prepare to finish another passage, but would first have to thank someone for the pair of setters she had just brought him, park them in the bedroom, return to accept his benefactress's invitation to lunch, run out again at Louise's cries, venture to say that it was certainly possible the setters had not been trained to live in an apartment, and lead them to the shower room where they set up such a constant howling that in the end no one paid any attention. Now and then, above the visitors' heads, Jonas glimpsed the look in Louise's eyes and thought she seemed sad. The end of the day would arrive at last, the visitors would take their leave, others would linger in the large room and look on fondly as Louise put the children to bed, with the kind help of an elegant lady in a hat who was terribly sorry to have to return at once to her two-story town house, where life was so much less cozy and intimate than at the Jonas household.

One Saturday afternoon Rateau came to bring Louise an ingenious clothes dryer that could be attached to the kitchen ceiling. He found the apartment full to bursting and in the small room, surrounded by art lovers, Jonas was painting the lady of the dogs, while being painted himself by an official artist. This person, according to Louise, was executing a state commission. "It will be called *The Artist at Work*." Rateau withdrew to a corner of the room to watch his friend, visibly absorbed by his effort. One of the art lovers, who had never seen Rateau, leaned toward him: "Hey," he said, "he looks good!" Rateau did not reply. "You paint?" the other man continued. "Me too. Ah well, believe me, he's on the way out."

"Already?" Rateau asked.

"Yes. It's success. No one can resist success. He's finished."

"He's on the way out or he's finished?"

"An artist who's on the way out is finished. Look, he has nothing to paint anymore. Now they're painting him and they'll hang him on the wall."

Later, in the middle of the night, in the bedroom, Louise, Rateau, and Jonas, who stood while the other two sat on a corner of the bed, were quiet. The children were sleeping, the dogs were at a kennel in the country, Louise had just washed up all the dishes, which Jonas and Rateau had dried, and their fatigue felt good.

"Hire a housekeeper," Rateau had said, looking at the pile of dishes. But Louise said sadly:

"Where would we put her?"

So they were quiet.

"Are you happy?" Rateau suddenly asked. Jonas smiled, but he looked weary.

"Yes. Everyone is kind to me."

"No," said Rateau. "Watch out. They're not all good."

"Who?"

"Your painter friends, for instance."

"I know," said Jonas. "But many artists are like that. They're not sure they exist, even the greatest. So they look for proof, they judge, they condemn. It bolsters them, it's the beginning of existence. They're so alone!"

Rateau shook his head.

"Believe me," Jonas said, "I know them. You have to love them."

"And what about you," said Rateau, "Do you exist, then? You never speak ill of anyone."

Jonas began to laugh:

"Oh, I often think ill of them. Only then I forget." He grew serious:

"No, I'm not certain I exist. But one day I will, I'm sure of that."

Rateau asked Louise what she thought. She emerged from her fatigue to say that Jonas was right: their visitors' opinions were not important. Only Jonas's work mattered. And she felt that the baby was in his way. Besides, he was growing, they needed to buy a little bed, and that would take up space. What could be done until they found a larger apartment? Jonas looked around the bedroom. Of course it was not ideal; the bed was very big. But the room was empty all day. He said this to Louise, who thought for a moment. In this room at least Jonas would not be disturbed; surely visitors wouldn't dare stretch out on their bed. "What do you think?" Louise asked Rateau. He looked at Jonas. Jonas was contemplating the windows across the way. Then he raised his eyes toward the starless sky and went to draw the curtains. When he returned, he smiled at Rateau and sat down beside him on the bed without saying anything. Louise, clearly exhausted, declared that she was going to take her shower. When the two friends were alone, Jonas felt Rateau's shoulder touch his. He did not look at him but said:

"I love to paint. I would like to paint all my life, day and night. Isn't that lucky?"

Rateau looked at him fondly:

"Yes," he said, "it's lucky."

The children were growing up and Jonas was happy to see them cheerful and vigorous. They were now in school and returned at four o'clock. Jonas still had them on Saturday afternoons, Thursdays, and also whole days during the long and frequent vacations. They were not yet big enough to play quietly, but were sturdy enough to fill the apartment with their squabbles and their laughter. They needed to be calmed, warned, sometimes threatened with a slap. There was also underwear to keep clean, buttons to sew on; Louise could no longer manage alone. Since they couldn't have a live-in housekeeper, or even bring such a person into the close intimacy of their living quarters, Jonas suggested appealing for help to Louise's sister, Rose, who had been left a widow with a grown daughter.

"Yes," said Louise, "with Rose, we won't be inconvenienced. We can tell her to leave when we like."

Jonas was pleased with this solution, which would relieve both Louise and his own conscience, as he was embarrassed by his wife's fatigue. The relief was even greater since the sister often brought her daughter along for reinforcement. The two of them were as good-hearted as could be: their decent natures radiated virtue and selflessness. They did whatever they could to come to the aid of the household, and never checked the clock. They were encouraged in this task by the tedium of their solitary lives and their pleasure in the ease they found at Louise's. As foreseen, indeed, no one was inconvenienced, and from the first day the two relatives felt at home. The large room became a common room, at once dining room, laundry room, and nursery. The small room, where the youngest child slept, served as a storeroom for canvases and a camp bed where Rose sometimes slept when she came without her daughter.

Jonas occupied the master bedroom and worked in the space that separated the bed from the window. He merely had to wait for the room to be made up in the morning, after the children's room was done. Then, no one would come to disturb him except to look for bed linen or towels, for the only armoire in the house was in this room. As for the visitors, although fewer in number, they already had their habits and, contrary to Louise's hope, did not hesitate to stretch out on the double bed, the better to chat with Jonas. The children would also come in to greet their father, saying, "Show us the picture." Jonas would show them the picture he was painting and kiss them fondly. Sending them off again, he felt that they took up all the space in his heart, fully, unconditionally. Deprived of them, he would find nothing but emptiness and solitude. He loved them as much as his painting because they alone in all the world were as alive as it was.

Yet Jonas was working less, without quite knowing why. He had always followed his routine, but now he had difficulty painting, even in moments of solitude. He would spend these moments looking at the sky. He had always been distracted and absorbed, but now he became a dreamer. He would think about painting, about his vocation, instead of painting. "I love to paint," he still said to himself, and the hand holding the paintbrush would hang at his side as he listened to a distant radio.

At the same time his reputation waned. People brought him articles that contained reservations, some that were plainly negative, and some that were so nasty his heart ached. But he told himself that there was also something to be gained from such attacks, which would incite him to work better. Those who continued to come treated him with less deference, like an old friend one needn't coddle. When he wanted to return to his work, they would say, "Come on, you've got plenty of time!" Jonas felt that in a certain sense they were already assimilating him to their own failure. But in another sense this new solidarity was in some way beneficial. Rateau shrugged his shoulders: "You're such a fool. They don't really love you."

"They still love me a little," Jonas replied. "A little love is a great thing. It doesn't matter how you get it!"

He continued to talk this way, writing letters and painting as best he could. Now and then he really painted, especially on Sunday afternoons when the children went out with Louise and Rose. On those evenings he rejoiced at having made a little progress on the unfinished picture. During this period he was painting skies.

On the day the dealer told him that, much to his regret, a clear decline in sales obliged him to reduce the monthly stipend, Jonas agreed but Louise expressed some anxiety. It was the month of September, the children needed clothes for the new school year. She set to work with her customary courage, and was soon overwhelmed. Rose, who could mend and sew on buttons, was not really a seamstress. But her husband's cousin was; she came to help Louise. From time to time she would settle in Jonas's room, in a corner chair, where this silent lady kept very still. So still was she that Louise suggested Jonas do a painting: *Woman at Work.* "Good idea," said Jonas. He tried, ruined two canvases, then went back to a sky he had begun. The following day he walked back and forth in the apartment and meditated instead of painting. A disciple, all worked up, came to show him a long article he would not otherwise have read, in which he learned that his painting was at once overrated and outdated; the dealer telephoned again to express his concern at the decline in sales. Yet Jonas continued to dream and meditate. He told the disciple that there was some truth in the article, but that he, Jonas, could still count on many years of work. To the dealer he replied that he understood his concern, but did not share it. He had a great work to do, something truly new; everything was going to begin again. As he talked he felt that what he said was true, and that his star was still there. All he needed was a good household arrangement.

On the days that followed he first tried to work in the hall, the day after that in the shower room under electric light, the next day in the kitchen. But for the first time he was bothered by the people he encountered everywhere, those he hardly knew and his own family, whom he loved. He stopped working for a while and meditated. He would have painted a seasonal subject if the weather were better. Unfortunately,

winter was about to begin, it would be difficult to do a landscape before spring. He tried, however, and gave up: the cold
chilled him to the bone. He lived several days with his canvases, most often sitting beside them, or standing motionless
in front of the window. He was not painting anymore. Then
he started going out in the morning. He would devise a
project to sketch a detail, a tree, a crooked house, a profile
glimpsed in passing. By the end of the day, he had done nothing. The slightest temptation—the newspapers, a chance
meeting, the shop windows, the warmth of a café—held him
spellbound. By evening he had no good excuse to assuage his
lingering bad conscience. He was going to paint, that was
certain, and paint better, after this period of apparent emptiness. The work was going on inside, that's all, the star would
emerge again, washed clean and sparkling, from this dark fog.
Meanwhile, he haunted the cafés. He had discovered that
alcohol gave him the same exaltation as those days of good
work when he used to think of his painting with that tenderness and warmth he had never felt for anything but his children. With the second cognac he rediscovered the poignant
emotion that made him at once the world's master and its ser-
vant. Simply he enjoyed it in a vacuum, his hands idle, without putting it into a work. Still, this was where he came
closest to the joy he lived for, and he now spent long hours
sitting, dreaming in smoke-filled, noisy places.

Yet he avoided the haunts and the neighborhoods fre-
quented by artists. When he met an acquaintance who spoke
to him about his painting he was seized with panic. He

wanted to flee, that was obvious, and he fled. He knew what people were saying behind his back: "He thinks he's Rembrandt," and his discomfort grew. He did not smile anymore, and his old friends drew an odd but inevitable conclusion from this: "If he doesn't smile anymore, it's because he's so pleased with himself." Knowing this, he became more and more evasive and skittish. He had only to enter a café and feel that someone there recognized him, and everything would go black inside him. For a moment he would stand stock still, filled with helplessness and a strange sorrow, his closed face concealing his unease, as well as his avid and abiding need for friendship. He would think of Rateau's friendly gaze, and he would leave abruptly. "Talk about a sad sack!" someone said one day, right next to him, as he was leaving.

He now visited only the outlying neighborhoods where no one knew him. There he could talk and smile, his benevolence was returned, no one asked anything of him. He made a few undemanding friends. He particularly liked the company of a waiter at a train station buffet where he often went. This waiter had asked him what he did for a living. "Painter," Jonas had replied. "Artist painter or house painter?"—"Artist."—"Ah well!" the man had said, "that's hard." And they never discussed the subject again. Yes it was hard, but Jonas was going to manage it once he had figured out how to organize his work.

Drinking day after day brought other chance encounters: women helped him. He could talk to them, before or after lovemaking, and above all boast a little, for they would understand him even if they were not convinced. Sometimes he felt his old strength returning. One day when he had been encouraged by one of his lady friends, he made a firm decision. He went home and tried to work again in the bedroom—the seamstress wasn't there. But after an hour he stowed his canvas, smiled at Louise without seeing her, and went out. He drank the entire day and spent the night at his friend's, without really feeling any desire for her. In the morning a living pain with its ravaged face received him in the person of Louise. She wanted to know if he had slept with this woman. And for the first time he saw on Louise's face that despair caused by surprise and an excess of pain, and it broke his heart. He discovered then that he had not thought about her all this time, and he was ashamed. He begged her forgiveness, it was over, tomorrow everything would begin again as before. Louise could not speak and turned away to hide her tears.

The next day Jonas went out very early. It was raining. When he came home, wet as a dog, he was loaded down with wooden boards. At his apartment two old friends, come for a visit, were drinking coffee in the large room. "Jonas is changing his technique. He is going to paint on wood!" they said. Jonas smiled: "It's not that. But I am beginning something new." He reached the little hallway that led to the shower room, the toilets, and the kitchen. In the right angle where the halls joined, he stopped and considered at length the high walls that rose to the dark ceiling. He needed a stepladder, and went downstairs to borrow one from the concierge.

When he climbed back upstairs there were a few more

people at his apartment, and he had to struggle against the affection of his visitors, delighted to find him in again, and against his family's questions, in order to reach the end of the hall. His wife was just coming out of the kitchen. Jonas, setting down his stepladder, hugged her close. Louise was looking at him: "I beg you," she said, "don't do it again."

"No, no," said Jonas. "I'm going to paint. I must paint." But he seemed to be talking to himself, his gaze was elsewhere. He set to work. Halfway up the walls he built a floor to form a kind of narrow loft, both high and deep. By the end of the afternoon, everything was finished. With the help of the stepladder, Jonas hung on to the floor of the loft and, to test the solidity of his work, did a few pull-ups. Then he mingled with the others and everyone was delighted to find him so friendly again. That evening, when the house was relatively empty, Jonas took an oil lamp, a chair, a stool, and a frame. He took everything up to the loft before the bewildered gaze of three women and the children. "There," he said from the height of his perch. "Now I'll work without bothering anyone." Louise asked if he was sure about this. "Yes, of course," he said, "I don't need much space. I'll be freer, there were great painters who painted by candlelight, and . . ." "Is the floor solid?" It was. "Don't worry," said Jonas, "it's a very good solution." And he came down again.

The next day, as early as possible, he climbed up to the loft, sat down, placed the frame on the stool against the wall, and waited without lighting the lamp. The only noises he heard clearly were coming from the kitchen or the toilet. Other sounds seemed distant, and the visits, the ringing of the doorbell or the telephone, the comings and goings, the conversations reached him half-muffled, as if they were coming from the street or from the other courtyard. Besides, when the whole apartment was flooded with a harsh light, the darkness here was restful. From time to time a friend would come and camp beneath the loft. "What are you doing up there, Jonas?"—"I'm working."—"Without light?"—"Yes, for the time being." He was not painting, but he was meditating. In the darkness and this half silence which, compared to his previous experience, seemed to him the silence of the desert or the grave, he was listening to his own heart. The sounds that reached the loft did not seem to concern him now, even if they were addressed to him. He was like those men who die at home alone in their sleep, and when morning comes the telephone rings and keeps ringing, urgent and insistent, in the deserted house, over a corpse forever deaf. But he was alive, he was listening to this silence within himself, he was waiting for his star, still hidden but ready to rise again, to emerge at last, unchanged, above the disorder of these empty days. "Shine, shine," he would say. "Don't deprive me of your light." It would shine again, he was sure of it. But he still needed more time to meditate, since at last he had the chance to be alone without being separated from his family. He needed to discover what he had not yet clearly understood, although he had always known it, and had always painted as if he knew it. He had to grasp at long last that secret which was not merely the secret of art, he could see. That is why he did not light the lamp.

Each day now Jonas climbed back up to his loft. The visitors were fewer because Louise was preoccupied and rarely engaged in conversation. Jonas would come down for meals and climb back to his perch. There he sat still in the dark all day. At night, he rejoined his wife, who was already asleep. At the end of a few days, he asked Louise to please give him his lunch, which she did with a care that touched Jonas deeply. So as not to bother her on other occasions, he suggested she prepare some provisions that he could store in the loft. As time went by, he no longer came back down during the day. But he hardly touched his provisions.

One evening he called Louise and asked for some blankets: "I'm going to spend the night here." Louise looked at him, her head tilted back. She opened her mouth, then shut it. She merely examined Jonas with a sad and worried expression; he suddenly saw how much she had aged, and how deeply the wear and tear of their life had affected her too. He realized that he had never really helped her. But before he could speak, she smiled at him with a tenderness that wrung his heart. "As you like, my dear," she said.

Afterward, he spent his nights in the loft and almost never came down. As a result, the apartment emptied of its visitors since they could no longer see Jonas, either day or night. Some said that he was in the country, others, tired of lying, that he had found a studio. Only Rateau came faithfully. He would climb up on the stepladder until his kind, intelligent face reached above the level of the floor: "How are you?" he would say.—"Couldn't be better."—"Are you working?"—"It amounts to the same thing."—"But you have no canvas!"—"I'm working anyway." It was difficult to sustain this dialogue from stepladder to loft. Rateau would shake his head, climb back down, help Louise repair the plumbing or fix a lock, then, without climbing on the stepladder, say goodnight to Jonas, who would answer from the darkness: "So long, my friend." One evening, Jonas added a thanks to his farewell. "Why thanks?"—"Because you love me."—"Big news!" said Rateau and he left.

Another evening Jonas called Rateau, who came running. The lamp was lit for the first time. Jonas was leaning out of the loft with an anxious expression. "Pass me a canvas," he said.—"But what's going on? You're so thin, you look like a ghost."—"I've hardly eaten for a couple of days. It's nothing, I must work."—"Eat first."—"No, I'm not hungry." Rateau brought a canvas. As he was about to disappear into the loft, Jonas asked him: "How are they?"—"Who?"—"Louise and the children."—"They're all right. They'd be better if you were with them."—"I'm not leaving them. Be sure to tell them, I'm not leaving them." And he disappeared. Rateau came to tell Louise he was worried. She admitted that she had been tormenting herself for several days. "What can we do? Oh, if only I could work in his place!" Miserable, she faced Rateau. "I can't live without him," she said. She looked like a young girl again, which surprised Rateau. Then he saw that she had blushed.

The lamp stayed lit all night and all morning the next day. To those who came, Rateau or Louise, Jonas said only: "Leave me alone, I'm working." At noon he asked for kerosene. The flickering lamp shone brightly again until evening. Rateau stayed for dinner with Louise and the children. At midnight, he went to say goodnight to Jonas. He waited a moment below the lighted loft, then left without a word. On the morning of the second day, when Louise got up, the lamp was still lit.

A beautiful day was dawning, but Jonas did not notice. He had turned the canvas to the wall. Exhausted, he was waiting, sitting with his hands open on his knees. He told himself that now he would never work again, he was happy. He heard his children shouting, the water running, the dishes clinking. Louise was talking. The huge windows rattled as a truck passed on the boulevard. The world was still there, young, lovable: Jonas listened to the lovely murmur of humanity. From so far away it did not conflict with that joyful strength in him, his art, those thoughts that he could never express but that set him above all things, in an atmosphere that was free and alive. The children were running through the rooms, the little girl was laughing, and Louise, too—he hadn't heard her laughter for a long time. He loved them! How he loved them! He put out the lamp, and in the familiar darkness wasn't that his star still shining? It was, he recognized it, his heart full of gratitude, and he was still gazing at it when he fell, noiselessly.

"It's nothing," the doctor who was called in declared some time later. "He's working too much. He'll be on his feet in a week."—"He will get well, you're quite sure?" said Louise, her face haggard.—"He will get well." In the other room, Rateau was looking at the canvas. It was entirely blank, though in the center Jonas had written in very small characters one word, which could be deciphered, but it was hard to tell whether it should be read as *independent* or *interdependent*.

The Growing Stone

The car veered heavily along the muddy, red dirt path. Suddenly, first on one side, then on the other, the headlights picked out two wooden shacks covered with corrugated iron. Near the second one, on the right, a tower built of crude beams could be glimpsed in the light fog. From the top of the tower a metal cable emerged, invisible at its starting point but glittering as it descended into the headlights' glare before disappearing behind the embankment that blocked the road. The car slowed down and stopped a few meters from the shacks.

The man who got out on the driver's right had difficulty extricating himself from the car. Once on his feet, he swayed a little on his colossal body. In the darkness near the car, sagging with fatigue and planted heavily on the ground, he seemed to be listening to the idling motor. Then he walked in the direction of the embankment and entered the cone of light from the headlights. He stopped at the top of the slope, his huge back outlined against the night. After a moment he turned around. The driver's black face gleamed above the dashboard, smiling. The man signaled; the driver cut the motor. At once, a great cool silence fell over the road and the forest. Then they heard the sound of water.

The man looked at the river down below, indicated only by a vague broad movement flecked with shiny scales. A denser motionless darkness, far off, must have been the other bank. Looking steadily, however, one could glimpse on that motionless bank a yellowish flame, like the eye of an oil lamp in the distance. The colossus turned toward the car and nodded his head. The driver switched off his headlights, turned them on again, then blinked them at regular intervals. On the embankment the man appeared and disappeared, taller and more massive at every resurrection. Suddenly, on the other side of the river, at the end of an invisible arm, a lantern was raised several times. At a final sign from the man watching, the driver switched off his headlights for good. The car and the man disappeared in the night. With the headlights off, the river was almost visible, or at least some of its long, liquid muscles shone intermittently. From each side of the path, the dark masses of the forest were outlined against the sky and seemed to loom near. The fine rain that had soaked the path an hour before still floated in the humid air, weighing on the silence and stillness of this large clearing in the middle of virgin forest. Misty stars flickered in the black sky.

But from the other bank rose the sound of chains, and

muffled lapping. Above the shack, to the right of the man still waiting there, the cable tightened. A muffled creaking began to run along it, while a faint surge of churning water rose from the river. The creaking leveled off, the sound of the water grew more pervasive, then became clearer as the lantern loomed. Now the yellowish halo surrounding it could be clearly seen. The halo gradually dilated and contracted again, as the lantern shone through the mist and began to illuminate a kind of square roof of dried palm leaves, supported at its four corners by thick bamboo posts. This crude shed, with vague shadows moving around it, was slowly approaching the bank. One could see midway across the river three small, dark men, naked to the waist and wearing conical hats, distinctly outlined by the yellow light. They stood motionless on their slightly parted legs, their bodies leaning a little to compensate for the drift of the river, pressing with all its invisible waters on the side of a large, crude raft that emerged from the night and the water. As the ferry came still closer, the man could make out behind the shed, on the downstream side, two tall blacks wearing only broad straw hats and gray cotton trousers. Side by side they leaned with all their might on the long poles that sank slowly into the river toward the back of the raft, while with the same slow motion they leaned above the waters as far as their balance allowed. In the front, the three mulattoes, motionless and silent, watched the bank approach without raising their eyes toward the man who was waiting for them.

The ferry suddenly knocked against the end of a wharf that extended into the water and was only now revealed by the lantern, which had begun to sway with the shock. The tall Negroes stood still, their hands above their heads, gripping the ends of the poles, which were barely dug in, but their tense muscles quivered constantly, as if from the water itself and its weight. The other ferrymen threw chains around the wharf posts, jumped onto the boards, and pulled down a sort of crude plank that covered the front of the raft with an inclined plane.

The man came back toward the car and climbed in as the driver started his engine. The car slowly climbed the embankment, pointed its hood toward the sky, then lowered it toward the river and tackled the downward slope. With the brakes on, it rolled and slid a little on the mud, stopping and starting. It crossed the wharf in a racket of jolting boards, reaching the end where the mulattoes, still silent, stood on either side, and plunged gently toward the raft. The raft dipped its nose in the water when the front wheels reached it and almost immediately resurfaced to receive the car's full weight. Then the driver kept his machine running until they reached the square roof at the back where the lantern hung. Instantly, the mulattoes refolded the inclined plank back onto the wharf and jumped with a single movement onto the ferry, at the same time pushing it off from the muddy bank. The river braced itself under the raft and raised it on the surface of the waters where it drifted slowly to the end of the long rail that was now running in the sky along a cable. The tall Negroes relaxed their efforts and brought up the poles. The man and the driver got out of the car and came to stand motionless on

the edge of the raft, facing upstream. No one had spoken during this maneuver, and even now each man stood in his place,
still and silent, except one of the tall Negroes, who was rolling
a cigarette in coarse paper.

The man was looking at the gap where the river surged
out of the great Brazilian forest and swept toward them. Several hundred centimeters wide at this place, the river's opaque
and silky waters pressed against the side of the ferry, then,
loosed at both ends, flowed over it and spread out again in a
single powerful flood running gently through the dark forest
toward the sea and the night. An unpleasant odor, coming
from the water or the spongy sky, floated on the air. Now the
lapping of the heavy waters under the ferry could be heard,
and from both banks the intermittent calls of the buffalo toads
or the strange cries of birds. The colossus walked over to the
driver. The small, thin man, leaning against one of the bamboo posts, stuck his fists in the pockets of his overalls, once
blue but now covered with the red dust they'd swallowed
during their daylong drive. A smile spread over his face, which
was lined despite his youth, and he was looking distractedly at
the fading stars still swimming in the damp sky.

But the birds' cries were clearer, mingled with strange
chattering, and almost instantly the cable began to creak. The
tall Negroes sunk their poles into the water and groped
blindly for the bottom. The man turned toward the shore they
had just left. Now it was covered by the darkness and the
waters, vast and savage like the continent of trees that stretched
beyond them for thousands of kilometers. Between the nearby

ocean and this sea of vegetation, the handful of men drifting at this hour on a savage river seemed lost. When the raft struck the new wharf, it was as if, having cast off all moorings, they had reached an island in the dark after days of terrifying navigation.

After landing, they heard the men's voices at last. The driver had just paid them, and in the heavy night, in strangely cheerful tones, they said farewell in Portuguese as the car started up again.

"They said sixty, the kilometers to Iguape. Three hours you drive and it's over. Socrates is happy," the driver announced.

The man laughed, a good laugh, hearty and warm, like him.

"Me too, Socrates—I'm happy, too. The road is hard."

"Too heavy, Monsieur d'Arrast, you too heavy," and the driver was laughing, too, as if he couldn't stop.

The car had picked up a little speed. It was moving between high walls of trees and tangled vegetation, amidst a faint sugary smell. The crisscrossing flights of fireflies passed constantly through the darkness of the forest, and every once in a while birds with red eyes would knock against the windshield for a moment. Sometimes, a strange growling would reach them from the depths of the night, and the driver would look at his passenger, comically rolling his eyes.

The road looped back and forth, crossing small streams over bridges of rattling planks. At the end of an hour, the mist began to thicken. A fine drizzle began to fall, dimming the headlights. Despite the jolting, d'Arrast was half-asleep. He was no longer driving in the damp forest but on the roads of the Sierra, which they had taken that morning as they left São Paulo. The red dust they could still taste in their mouths rose without respite from those dirt tracks, and on every side, as far as they could see, it covered the sparse vegetation of the plains. The heavy sun, the pale mountains full of ravines, the scrawny zebus encountered on the roads with a red flight of ragged urubus as their only escort, the long, long navigation across a red desert . . . He gave a start. The car had stopped. They were now in Japan: fragile houses on either side of the road, and in the houses, furtive kimonos. The driver was talking to a Japanese man wearing dirty overalls and a Brazilian straw hat. The car started again.

"He said only forty kilometers."

"Where were we? In Tokyo?"

"No, Registro. In our country, all the Japanese end up there."

"Why?"

"Don't know. They're yellow, you know, Monsieur d'Arrast."

But the forest was clearing a little, the road was easier, if still slippery. The car was skidding on the sand. A damp breeze, warm and slightly sharp, blew through the car window.

"Smell it?" the driver said eagerly "it's the good sea. Soon Iguape."

"If we have enough gas," d'Arrast replied.

And he went peacefully back to sleep.

———

Sitting up in bed after waking early the next morning, d'Arrast looked around the room in surprise. The lower half of the high walls was freshly painted a chalky brown. They had once been painted white above, and now shreds of yellowish crusts covered them up to the ceiling. Two rows of six beds faced each other. D'Arrast saw only one bed unmade at the end of his row, and this bed was empty. But he heard some noise to his left and turned toward the door, where Socrates, a bottle of mineral water in each hand, stood laughing.

"Happy memory!" he was saying. D'Arrast shook himself. Yes, the hospital where the mayor had lodged them the evening before was called Happy Memory. "Sure memory," Socrates continued. "They told me first build the hospital, later build water. While waiting, happy memory, have some bubbly water to wash up." He disappeared, laughing and singing, not in the least exhausted, it seemed, by the cataclysmic sneezes that had shaken him all night and had kept d'Arrast from closing his eyes.

Now d'Arrast was fully awake. Through the grill work on the windows across the room he could see a little courtyard of red earth soaked by the rain that could be seen noiselessly dripping on a bunch of tall aloes. A woman passed by, raising a yellow scarf above her head. D'Arrast lay down again, then sat up at once and got out of the bed, which buckled and groaned beneath his weight. Socrates entered at the same moment: "For you, Monsieur d'Arrast. The mayor is waiting outside." But seeing d'Arrast's expression, he added: "Don't worry, he's never in a hurry."

After shaving in mineral water, d'Arrast went out onto the porch of the pavilion. The mayor—who was slim and under his round, gold-rimmed glasses looked like a friendly weasel—seemed absorbed in gloomy contemplation of the rain. But a delighted smile transfigured him as soon as he saw d'Arrast. Straightening his small body, he hurried over and tried to throw his arms around "Monsieur Engineer." At that moment, a car began to brake in front of them on the other side of the low wall of the court, skidded in the damp clay, and came to a lopsided halt. "The judge!" said the mayor. The judge, like the mayor, was dressed in navy blue. But he was much younger, or at least seemed to be because of his elegant figure and his fre~~sh f~~ _ ~~i l d l like~~ a surprised adolescent. He was cros~~s~~ ~~their~~ direction, gracefully avoiding th~~ few steps away from d'Arrast, he was a~~ ~~arms~~ and bidding him welcome. He wa~~ ~~Monsieur~~ Engineer, who was bestowing s~~ ~~for~~ town; the judge was thrilled at the~~ engineer would ren~~der Iguape by constructing this little dam that would prevent the periodic flooding of the town's riverside quarters. To command the waters, to conquer rivers, ah!—a great profession, and surely the poor people of Iguape would remember the engineer's name and for many years to come would still utter it in their prayers. D'Arrast, captivated by such charm and eloquence, thanked him and didn't dare ask what a judge had to do with a dam. Besides, according to the mayor, he had to visit the club where the town dignitaries wanted to give

Monsieur Engineer a worthy welcome before he could visit the poorer quarters. Who were these dignitaries?

"Ah, well," said the mayor, "myself, as mayor, Monsieur Carvalho, here, the captain of the port, and several other less important men. Anyway, you won't have to bother about them, they don't speak French."

D'Arrast called Socrates and told him that he would look for him at the end of the morning.

"Yes, okay," said Socrates. "I'll go to the Jardin de la Fontaine."

"To the Jardin?"

"Yes, everyone knows it. Don't worry, Monsieur d'Arrast."

The hospital, d'Arrast saw on his way out, was built at the edge of the forest, whose massive foliage cascaded almost to the roofs. On every surface of the trees a fine veil of water was falling, which the thick forest was noiselessly absorbing, like an enormous sponge. The town, some hundred houses covered with faded tile roofs, extended between the forest and the river, whose distant murmur reached as far as the hospital. The car entered the rain-soaked streets and came out almost at once onto a rectangular, rather large square, which preserved in its red clay between numerous puddles the traces of tires, iron wheels, and horseshoes. All around, low houses covered with multicolored plaster enclosed the square, and behind it could be seen the two round blue and white towers of the colonial-style church. Against this stark backdrop floated a salty smell from the estuary. In the middle of the square several drenched silhouettes were wandering. A motley crowd of gauchos, Japanese, half-breed Indians, and elegant

dignitaries, whose dark suits seemed exotic here, were strolling slowly with leisurely gestures past the houses. They
stepped aside, in an unhurried fashion, to make way for the
car, then stopped and gazed after it. When the car stopped in
front of one of the houses on the square, a circle of wet gauchos silently surrounded it.

At the club—a kind of little bar on the second floor furnished with a bamboo counter and iron café tables—the dignitaries were numerous. They drank cane liquor in d'Arrast's
honor after the mayor, drink in hand, had welcomed him
and wished him all the best. But while d'Arrast was drinking
near the window, a tall beanpole of a fellow in riding breeches
and leggings came staggering up to deliver a rapid and
obscure speech, in which the engineer recognized only the
word *passport*. He hesitated, then took out the document
which the other fellow grabbed voraciously. After leafing
through the passport, the beanpole displayed his bad temper.
He resumed his speech, shaking the passport under the nose
of the engineer, who, without much emotion, merely looked
at the furious man. Just then the judge, smiling, came over to
ask what the matter was. For a moment the drunk examined
the frail creature who had dared to interrupt him then, staggering even more dangerously, shook the passport in the face
of this new listener. D'Arrast sat peacefully beside a table and
waited. The dialogue became very lively, and suddenly, to his
surprise, the judge let loose with a deafening voice. Unpre-
dictably, the beanpole beat an abrupt retreat with the look of a
child caught in the act. At a final order from the judge, he

headed toward the door, moving sidelong like a scolded dunce, and disappeared.

The judge immediately came over to explain to d'Arrast, in a voice once again harmonious, that this uncouth character was the chief of police, that he had dared to claim the passport was not in order, and would be punished for his misdemeanor. Monsieur Carvalho then addressed the dignitaries, who were circled around, and seemed to be asking their opinions. After a short discussion, the judge expressed solemn apologies to d'Arrast, urged him to grant that only drunkenness could explain such an abysmal lack of respect and gratitude, which the entire town of Iguape owed him, and finally begged him to be so good as to decide himself on the punishment to be inflicted on this dreadful character. D'Arrast said that he did not want any punishment, that it was a trivial incident, and that he was in a particular hurry to go to the river. The mayor then spoke again to assert with fond good humor that really, a punishment was indispensable, that the guilty man would remain under arrest, and that they would wait, all of them, for their eminent visitor to be so good as to decide his fate. No protestations could sway this smiling severity, and d'Arrast had to promise that he would think about it. Afterward, they decided to visit the riverside quarters of the town.

The river was already spreading its yellowish waters on the low, glistening banks. They had left the last houses of Iguape behind them and were meandering between the river and a steep embankment, where huts of mud and branches clung. In front of them, at the end of the embankment, the forest began again without transition, as on the other bank. But the breach of the waters swiftly broadened between the trees up to an indistinct line, more gray than yellow, which marked the sea. Without saying a word, d'Arrast walked toward the slope, where the marks of various floodwaters were still fresh on its flank. A muddy path climbed toward the huts. In front of them, blacks stood silently watching the new-comers. Several couples were holding hands, and at the very edge of the embankment, in front of the adults, a row of little Negroes, their bellies bulging over skinny legs, stared round-eyed.

Reaching the front of the huts, d'Arrast beckoned to the commander of the port. He was a fat, laughing black man dressed in a white uniform. D'Arrast asked him in Spanish if it were possible to visit a hut. The commander was certain of it, he even thought it a good idea, and Monsieur Engineer would see some very interesting things. He addressed the black men at length, pointing to d'Arrast and the river. They listened without a word. When the commander was finished, · no one moved. He spoke again, in an impatient voice. Then he asked one of the men, who shook his head. The com-mander said a few brief words then, in an imperative tone. The man detached himself from the group, stood in front of d'Arrast, and with a gesture showed him the way. But his gaze was hostile. He was an older man, his head covered with short grizzled wool, his face thin and shriveled; his body was still young, though, with hard spare shoulders and muscles visible under his cotton pants and torn shirt. They advanced, followed by the commander and the crowd of blacks, and climbed up a new, even steeper slope, where the huts of mud, tin, and reeds clung to the soil with such difficulty that their base had been shored up with big stones. They met a woman coming down the path, sometimes slipping on her bare feet, carrying an iron jug of water on her head. Then they arrived at a small, squarelike area formed by three huts. The man walked toward one of them and pushed open a bamboo door whose hinges were made of lianas. He stepped aside, without a word, fixing the engineer with the same impassive gaze. In the hut, d'Arrast saw nothing at first but a dying fire set right on the ground at the exact center of the room. Then he made out in a back corner a brass bed with a bare, broken frame, a table in the other corner covered with an earthenware dish, and between the two a sort of trestle where a color print representing Saint George held pride of place. For the rest, nothing but a heap of rags to the right of the entrance, and hanging from the ceiling a few colorful loincloths drying over the fire. Standing still, D'Arrast breathed in the odor of smoke and poverty that rose from the ground and caught him by the throat. Behind him the commander clapped his hands. The engineer turned around and on the threshold, against the daylight, he saw only the graceful silhouette of a young black girl holding something out to him: he took a glass and drank the thick cane liquor it contained. The young girl held out her tray to receive the empty glass and left with a movement so supple and lively that d'Arrast suddenly wanted to stop her.

But going out behind her, he didn't recognize her in the crowd of blacks and dignitaries gathered around the hut. He thanked the old man, who bowed his head without a word. Then he left. The commander behind him resumed his explanations, asked when the French company from Rio could begin the work and whether the dam would be built before the big rains. D'Arrast did not know, but wasn't really thinking about it. He went down toward the cool river, under the implacable rain. He was still listening to that great pervasive sound he had been hearing since his arrival: was it the rustling of the waters or the trees? Reaching the bank he looked at the distant, indefinite line of the sea, thousands of kilometers of solitary waters and Africa, and beyond that Europe, where he came from.

"Commander," he said, "these people we've just seen, what do they live on?"

"They work when they're needed," said the commander. "We are poor."

"Are these the poorest?"

"They are the poorest."

The judge, who arrived at that moment by gliding lightly on his fine soles, said that they already loved Monsieur Engineer, who was going to give them work.

"And you know," he said, "they dance and sing every day."

Then, without transition, he asked d'Arrast if he had thought of the punishment.

"What punishment?"

"Ah well, our chief of police."

"You should let him go." The judge said that this was not possible, and that he had to be punished. D'Arrast was already walking toward Iguape.

In the little Jardin de la Fontaine, mysterious and pleasant under the fine rain, clusters of exotic flowers cascaded along the lianas between the banana trees and the pandanus. Piles of wet stones marked the intersection of the paths where at this hour a motley crowd was circulating. Half-breeds, mulattoes, a few gauchos were chatting quietly or strolling farther on, as slowly as before, along the bamboo paths to the place where the groves and underbrush became thicker, then impenetrable. There, without transition, the forest began.

D'Arrast was looking for Socrates among the crowd when the man came up behind him. "It's a holiday," said Socrates, laughing, and leaned on d'Arrast's high shoulders to jump up.

"What holiday?"

"Ah!" Socrates was surprised and now faced d'Arrast. "You don't know? The holiday of the good Jesus. Each year, everyone comes to the grotto with a hammer."

Socrates was pointing not to a grotto, but to a group that seemed to be waiting in one corner of the public garden. "You see, one day the statue of the good Jesus, it came from the sea, floating down the river. Some fishermen found it. So beautiful! So beautiful! Then they washed it here in the grotto. And now a stone has grown in the grotto. Every year there's a holiday. With a hammer you break, you break off

pieces for a blessing. And then what happens? It keeps growing, you keep breaking. That's the miracle."

They had reached the grotto and could see its low
entrance above the waiting men. Inside, in darkness punctuated by flickering candle flames, a squatting figure was striking the stone with a hammer. The man, a thin gaucho with a
long mustache, stood up and came out, displaying in his open
palm a piece of damp schist. After a few moments, before
going away, he closed his hand on it as a precaution. Another
man then stooped and entered the grotto.

D'Arrast turned around. On every side pilgrims were
waiting, without looking at him, impassive beneath the water
that fell from the trees in thin veils. He too was waiting, in
front of the grotto, under the same film of water, and he did
not know for what. The truth is, he had not stopped waiting
since he had arrived in this country a month before. He was
waiting—in the red heat of humid days, under the tiny stars at
night, despite his tasks, the dams to build, the roads to cut
through—as if the work he had come here to do were merely
a pretext, the occasion for a surprise or an encounter he could
not even imagine, but that had been waiting for him, patiently,
at the end of the world. He pulled himself together, walked
away without anyone in the little group taking notice, and
headed toward the exit. He needed to return to the river and
go to work.

But Socrates was waiting for him at the entrance, lost in
voluble conversation with a short, sturdy man, with yellow
rather than black skin. The man's completely shaven head

made his nicely shaped forehead seem even broader. By contrast, his large, smooth face was adorned with a very black beard, trimmed square.

"This guy, the champion!" said Socrates by way of introduction. "Tomorrow, he makes the procession."

The man, dressed in a sailor's suit of rough serge, a blue-and-white-striped jersey under a nautical blouse, examined d'Arrast attentively with his calm, black eyes. At the same time he was smiling widely, showing his very white teeth between full, glistening lips.

"He speaks Spanish," Socrates said, and turning to the stranger:

"Tell Monsieur d'Arrast." Then he danced off toward another group. The man stopped smiling and looked at d'Arrast with frank curiosity.

"This interests you, Captain?"

"I'm not a captain," d'Arrast said.

"Never mind. But you're a lord. Socrates told me."

"Not me. But my grandfather was. His father too, and all those before his father. Now, there are no more lords in our countries."

"Ah!" the man said, laughing, "I understand, everyone is a lord."

"No, it's not that. There are neither lords nor commoners."

The other man reflected, then made up his mind:

"No one works, no one suffers?"

"Yes, millions of men."

"Then those are the common people."

"In that way, yes, there are common people. But their masters are the police and the tradesmen."

The mulatto's kind face closed up. Then he grumbled:

"Humph! Buying and selling, eh? What garbage! And with the police, the dogs are in command."

Without transition, he burst out laughing.

"You, you don't sell?"

"Hardly. I make bridges, roads."

"That's good! Me, I'm a ship's cook. If you want, I'll make you our dish of black beans."

"I'd like that."

The cook approached d'Arrast and took his arm.

"Listen, I like what you tell. I am going to tell you, too. You will like perhaps."

He led him near the entrance to a damp wooden bench beneath a stand of bamboo.

"I was at sea, in the waters off Iguape, on a little tanker that supplies shipping for the ports along the coast. There was a fire on board. Not by my fault, eh! I know my job! No, bad luck. We were able to put the lifeboats in the water. During the night, the sea rose, it overturned the lifeboat, and I fell out. When I came up, I knocked my head against the boat. I drifted. The night was dark, the waters are big and besides, I swim badly, I was afraid. All at once, I saw a light in the distance and recognized the dome of the church of the good Jesus in Iguape. Then I told the good Jesus that in the procession I would carry a stone of fifty kilos on my head if he saved me. You don't believe me, but the waters grew calm, and my heart too. I swam slowly, I was happy, and I reached the shore. Tomorrow I will keep my promise."

He looked at d'Arrast, suddenly suspicious.

"You're not laughing, eh?"

"I'm not laughing. A man has to do what he's promised."

The other clapped him on the shoulder.

"Now, come to my brother's place, near the river. I'll cook you some beans."

"No," d'Arrast said, "I have things to do. This evening, if you like."

"Good. But tonight we dance and pray in the big hut. It's the festival of Saint George." D'Arrast asked him if he was dancing too. The cook's face hardened all at once; for the first time, his eyes shifted away.

"No, no, I won't dance. Tomorrow I must carry the stone. It's heavy. I'll go this evening to celebrate the saint. And then I'll leave early."

"Does it last long?"

"All night, into early morning."

He looked at d'Arrast sheepishly.

"Come to the dance. And you will take me back afterward. Otherwise, I'll stay, I'll dance, I might not be able to stop myself."

"You like to dance?"

The cook's eyes shone with a sort of avidity.

"Oh, yes! I like. Besides, there are the cigars, the saints, the women. You forget everything, you let yourself go."

"There are women? All the women from the town?"

"From the town, no, but from the huts."

The cook smiled again.

"Come. I'll obey the captain. And you will help me keep my promise tomorrow."

D'Arrast felt vaguely annoyed. What did this ridiculous promise have to do .with him? But he looked at the handsome, open face that was smiling at him trustingly, and the yellow skin shining with health and vitality.

"I'll come," he said. "Now I'll walk along with you a bit."

Not knowing why, he could still see the young black girl holding out the welcome offering.

They left the garden, walked along several muddy streets, and arrived at the square full of potholes that looked larger because of the low houses surrounding it. The humidity was streaming down the plaster walls, although the rain had not intensified. Across the spongy expanse of the sky the muffled murmur of the river and the trees reached them. They were walking in step, d'Arrast heavily, the cook with an athletic stride. From time to time the man would raise his head and smile at his companion. They went in the direction of the church, which could be seen above the houses, reached the end of the square, then walked again along muddy streets suffused with aggressive cooking odors. Now and then a woman holding a plate or a cooking utensil showed a curious face in one of the doors and immediately disappeared. They passed in front of the church, plunged into an old quarter of town between the same low houses, and suddenly emerged at the sound of the invisible river, behind a neighborhood of huts that d'Arrast recognized.

"Good. I'll leave you. Till tonight," he said.

"Yes, in front of the church."

But the cook held on to d'Arrast's hand. He was hesitating. Then he made up his mind:

"And you, did you ever call out or make a promise?"

"Yes, once, I think."

"In a shipwreck?"

"If you like." And d'Arrast roughly pulled his hand away. But just as he was turning on his heels, he met the cook's gaze. He hesitated, then smiled.

"I can tell you, although it wasn't very important. Someone was about to die because of me. I think I called out."

"You promised?"

"No. I would have liked to promise."

"Was it a long time ago?"

"Just before coming here."

The cook took his beard in both hands. His eyes were shining.

"You are a captain," he said. "My house is yours. And then, you're going to help me keep my promise, it's as if you made it yourself. It will help you too."

D'Arrast smiled. "I don't think so."

"You're proud, Captain."

"I used to be proud, now I'm alone. But just tell me, has your good Jesus always answered you?"

"Always, no, Captain!"

"So then?"

The cook burst into fresh, childish laughter.

"Ah well," he said, "he's free, isn't he?"

At the club, where d'Arrast was lunching with the dignitaries, the mayor told him that he should sign the municipality's guest book at least as a testimony to the great event of his arrival in Iguape. The judge on his side found two or three new formulations to celebrate, in addition to their guest's virtues and talents, the simplicity with which he represented among them the great nation to which he had the honor to belong. D'Arrast said only that this was indeed an honor, he was sure, and also an advantage for his company to have won the bid for this big construction job. Once more the judge exclaimed at such humility. "By the way," he said, "have you thought of what we should do with the chief of police?" D'Arrast looked at him, smiling. "I have." He would consider it a personal favor, and an exceptional gesture, if they would be so good as to pardon this thoughtless person in his name, so that his stay here—his, d'Arrast's, as he was taking so much pleasure in getting acquainted with the lovely town of Iguape and its generous inhabitants—could begin in a climate of concord and friendship. The judge, attentive and smiling, nodded his head. As a connoisseur, he meditated a moment on this formulation, then called upon the audience to applaud the magnanimous traditions of the great French nation, and turning again toward d'Arrast, declared he was satisfied. "Since that's settled," he concluded, "we shall dine this evening with the chief." But d'Arrast said that he was invited by friends to attend the dance ceremony in the huts. "Ah, yes!" said the judge, "I am happy you are going. You will see one cannot help loving our people."

That evening, d'Arrast, the cook, and his brother were sitting around the remnants of the fire at the center of the hut, which the engineer had already visited that morning. The brother had not seemed surprised to see him again. He hardly spoke Spanish and mostly just nodded his head. As for the cook, he was interested in cathedrals, then spoke at length about the black bean soup. Now daylight was fading, and while d'Arrast could still see the cook and his brother, he had trouble making out at the back of the hut the squatting silhouettes of an old woman and the same young girl who had served him. Below, they could hear the monotonous river.

The cook stood up and said: "It's time." They rose, but the women did not move. The men went out alone. D'Arrast hesitated, then joined the others. Night had fallen now, the rain had stopped. The pale black sky still seemed liquid. In its dark, transparent water, low on the horizon, stars were beginning to flare. They flickered out almost at once, falling one by one into the river, as if the sky were spilling its last lights, drop by drop. The thick air smelled of water and smoke. And they could hear close by the murmur of the vast, motionless forest. Suddenly drums and chanting rose in the distance, at first muffled then distinct, coming closer and closer and then ceasing. Soon after, they saw a procession of black girls dressed in long white dresses of raw silk. Wearing a fitted red tunic and a necklace of colored teeth, a tall black man was following them, and behind him, a disorderly troop of men in white pajamas and musicians carrying triangles and broad, short drums. The cook said they should follow them.

Along the riverbank, several hundred meters from the last huts, they reached the large, empty hut, which with its plaster walls was relatively comfortable inside. There was a dirt floor, a roof of thatch and reeds supported by a central pole, and bare walls. On a little altar at the back lined with palm fronds and covered with candles that barely lit up half the hall, they glimpsed a wonderful color print in which Saint George, with seductive gestures, was getting the better of a mustached dragon. Beneath the altar in a sort of niche decorated with paper rocks, a little clay statue painted red, representing a horned god, stood between a candle and a bowl of water. The savage-looking god was brandishing an enormous sword made of silver paper.

The cook led d'Arrast to a corner where they stood leaning against the walls near the door. "This way," murmured the cook, "we can leave without disturbing." Indeed, the hut was full of men and women squeezed against each other. The heat was already rising. The musicians took their places on either side of the altar. The male and female dancers separated into two concentric circles, with the men on the inside. Into the center stepped the black leader in the red tunic. D'Arrast leaned against the walls, crossing his arms.

But the leader, cutting through the circle of dancers, came

toward them and gravely spoke a few words to the cook. "Uncross your arms, Captain," said the cook. "You're hugging yourself, you're preventing the saint's spirit from descending." Obediently, d'Arrast let his arms fall to his sides. Still leaning against the wall, with his long, heavy limbs, his large face already gleaming with sweat, he himself now resembled some bestial and reassuring god. The tall black man looked at him and then, satisfied, went back to his place. At once, in a ringing voice, he chanted the first notes of a melody that everyone took up in chorus, accompanied by the drums. The circles then began to turn in opposite directions in a kind of heavy, insistent dance rather more like stamping, lightly accented by the double swaying of hips.

The heat had increased. Yet the pauses gradually became less frequent, and the dance took off. Without slowing the others down, continuing to dance himself, the tall black man again cut through the circles toward the altar. He came back with a glass of water and a lit candle, which he stuck in the earth at the center of the hut. He poured the water around the candle in two concentric circles, and standing again, raised his wild eyes toward the roof. His whole body tense, he was waiting, motionless. "Saint George is coming. Look! Look!" whispered the cook, whose eyes were widening.

Indeed, several dancers seemed in a trancelike state, but a rigid trance, their hands at their sides, their steps stiff, eyes fixed and vacant. Others quickened their rhythm, convulsing backward, and began to utter inarticulate cries. The cries rose gradually and once they had mingled in a collective howl, the leader, his eyes still raised, gave a long, barely comprehensible shriek at the top of his lungs, in which some words kept recurring. "You see," whispered the cook, "he says that he is the god's battlefield." D'Arrast was struck by the change in his voice and looked at the cook, who, leaning forward, his fists clenched and his eyes staring, was stamping rhythmically in place like the others. He perceived, then, that for a moment, without moving his feet, he too had been dancing with all his weight.

But all at once the drums let loose and suddenly the tall red devil was unleashed. His eyes inflamed, his four limbs writhing around his body, he hopped first on one leg then on the other, bending his knees, his rhythm accelerating so fast it seemed he would surely come apart. But abruptly he stopped in full flight to look at the spectators with a proud and terrible expression as the drums thundered. Immediately a dancer leaped from a dark corner, knelt, and held out a short saber to the possessed man. The tall black leader took the saber without taking his eyes off the dancers around him, then whirled it above his head. At the same moment d'Arrast saw the cook who was dancing among the others. The engineer had not seen him move away.

In the reddish, uncertain light a stifling dust was rising from the ground, thickening the already heavy air that clung to the skin. D'Arrast felt gradually overcome by fatigue; it was harder and harder for him to breathe. He did not even see how the dancers had gotten the enormous cigars they were now smoking as they continued to dance, and whose strange odor filled the hut and made him dizzy. He saw only the cook who passed near him, always dancing, and also puffing on a cigar: "Don't smoke," he said. The cook grunted, without losing his rhythm, staring at the central pole with the expression of a groggy boxer, the nape of his neck constantly twitching with a long shudder. At his side, a stout black woman, moving her animal face from right to left, kept up a continuous barking. But the young Negro girls in particular were entering into the most terrifying trance, their feet glued to the ground and their bodies shuddering from head to foot in spasms that grew increasingly violent as they reached the shoulders. Their heads began to nod back and forth, as if separated from decapitated bodies. At the same time, everyone began to howl without letup, a long collective, toneless howl, seemingly without pause for breath or modulation, as if their bodies were entirely knotted together, muscles and nerves, in a single powerful outburst that at last gave voice in each of them to a being which had until then been absolutely silent.

And still howling, the women began to fall one by one. The black leader knelt beside each of them, quickly and convulsively pressing their temples with his big black muscled hand. Then they would stand up, stagger, begin to dance, and take up their cries once more, at first weakly, then ever faster and more high pitched, only to fall again, and get up again, begin once more, and for a long time still, until the general howl weakened, changed, degenerated into a sort of raucous, gulping bark that shook them all. D'Arrast, exhausted, his muscles in knots from his long motionless dance, suffocated by his own muteness, felt faint. The heat, the dust, the smoke of the cigars, the smell of human bodies was making the air completely unbreathable. He looked for the cook: he had disappeared. D'Arrast managed to slide along the walls and crouched over, feeling nauseous.

When he opened his eyes, the air was still stifling, but the noise had stopped. The drums alone were beating out a continuous bass, while in all the corners of the hut, groups of people covered with white fabric were stamping. But in the center of the room, now unencumbered by the glass and the candle, a group of young black girls in a semihypnotic state were dancing slowly, barely keeping up with the rhythm. Their eyes closed, yet still erect, they were swaying lightly back and forth on their toes, almost in place. Two fat girls had faces covered with a curtain of raffia. They stood on either side of another tall, slim young girl in costume, whom d'Arrast suddenly recognized as the daughter of his host. In a green dress and wearing a huntress's hat of blue gauze turned up in front and adorned with musketeer plumes, she held in her hand a green and yellow bow armed with an arrow, at the end of which a colorful bird was skewered. On her lithe body her pretty head rolled slowly, tilted back a little, and her sleeping face reflected both melancholy and innocence. Whenever the music halted, she staggered sleepily. The pounding rhythm of the drums alone acted as a kind of support around which she wrapped her languid arabesques until, once again pausing in time to the music, staggering at the edge of balance, she uttered a strange bird cry, piercing and yet melodious.

D'Arrast, entranced by this slow-motion dance, was watching the black Diana when the cook loomed before him, his smooth face now distorted. The goodwill had disappeared from his eyes, which reflected only a kind of unfamiliar avidity. Coldly, as if speaking to a stranger, he said: "It's late, Captain. They're going to dance all night, but they don't want you to stay now." With a heavy head, d'Arrast stood up and followed the cook, clinging along the walls to reach the door. On the threshold, the cook stepped aside, holding the bamboo door, and d'Arrast went out. He turned and looked at the cook, who had not moved. "Come on. Soon you'll have to carry the stone."

"I'm staying," the cook said firmly.

"And your promise?"

Without answering, the cook gradually pushed against the door as d'Arrast held it open with one hand. They remained this way for a moment until d'Arrast gave in, shrugging his shoulders. He walked away.

The night was full of fresh, aromatic scents. Above the forest, the few stars in the southern sky, blurred by an invisible mist, shone weakly. The humid air was heavy. Yet it seemed deliciously cool outside the hut. D'Arrast climbed up the muddy slope and reached the first huts, staggering like a drunk on the potholed paths. Close by, the forest was growling a little. The sound of the river grew louder, the whole continent was emerging in the night, and d'Arrast was overcome by nausea. It seemed to him that he would have liked to vomit up this whole country, the sadness of its great spaces, the murky light of its forest, and the nocturnal lapping of its great empty rivers. This land was too vast, blood and seasons mingled in it, time was liquefying. Life here was at ground level, and to be part of it one had to lie down and sleep for years on the muddy or parched earth. Over in Europe there was shame and fury. Here, exile or solitude among these list-less and throbbing madmen who were dancing to death. But through the humid night, full of vegetable scents, a wounded bird's strange cry, uttered by the beautiful sleepwalker, still reached him.

When d'Arrast, his head heavy with a crushing migraine, had wakened after a bad sleep, a humid heat was weighing upon the town and the motionless forest. At this moment he was waiting on the porch of the hospital looking at his watch, which had stopped; he was uncertain of the time, surprised by the broad daylight and the silence that rose from the town. The sky, an almost clear blue, hung on the first dull roofs. Yel-lowish urubus, transfixed by the heat, were sleeping on the houses across from the hospital. One of them suddenly shook itself, opened its beak, conspicuously prepared to fly, flapped its dusty wings twice against its body, rose a few centimeters above the roof, and fell back, going to sleep again almost instantly.

The engineer went down toward the town. The main square was deserted, like the streets he had just crossed. Far off, and from both sides of the river, a low mist floated over the forest. The heat was falling vertically, and d'Arrast looked for a scrap of shade where he could take refuge. Then he saw a little man gesturing to him under the awning of one of the houses. Coming closer, he recognized Socrates.

"So, Monsieur d'Arrast, you like the ceremony?"

D'Arrast said that it was too hot in the hut and that he preferred the sky and the night.

"Yes," Socrates said, "where you come from, it's only the mass. No one dances."

He rubbed his hands, jumped on one foot, spun around, laughing until he was breathless.

"Impossible, they're impossible."

Then he looked at d'Arrast with curiosity:

"And you, you go to mass?"

"No."

"So, where do you go?"

"Nowhere. I don't know."

Socrates was laughing again.

"Impossible! A lord without a church, without anything!"

D'Arrast was laughing too:

"Yes, you see, I never found my place. So I left."

"Stay with us, Monsieur d'Arrast, I love you."

"I'd like that, Socrates, but I don't know how to dance." Their laughter echoed in the silence of the empty town.

"Ah," Socrates said, "I forget. The mayor wants to see you. He is having lunch at the club." And without warning, he left in the direction of the hospital. "Where are you going?" d'Arrast called. Socrates imitated a snore: "To sleep. Soon the procession." And half running, he started his snoring again.

The mayor simply wanted to give d'Arrast a place of honor to watch the procession. He explained this to the engineer while making him share a plate of meat and rice fit for a regiment. First they would take their places on the balcony in the judge's house opposite the church to see the cortege come out. Then they would go to the town hall on the main street that the penitents would take on their return to the church square. The judge and the chief of police would accompany d'Arrast, the mayor being committed to participating in the ceremony. The chief of police was in fact in the room at the club and kept walking around d'Arrast, smiling continuously, lavishing him with incomprehensible but obviously benevolent words. When d'Arrast came down, the chief of police hurried to make way for him, holding all the doors open before him.

Under the intense sun, in the still empty town, the two men headed toward the judge's house. Their steps alone echoed in the silence. But suddenly a firecracker went off in a nearby street and caused the mangy-necked urubus to take flight in heavy, startled bunches on all the rooftops. Almost at once dozens of firecrackers went off in all directions, doors opened, and people began to leave the houses and fill the narrow streets.

The judge expressed to d'Arrast the pride he felt in welcoming him to his unworthy house and led him up one floor of a beautiful baroque staircase painted chalk blue. On the landing, as d'Arrast passed by, doors opened and filled with dark-haired children who then disappeared with muffled laughter. The main room, architecturally lovely, contained nothing but rattan furniture and large cages full of birds that kept up a deafening chatter. The balcony where they settled looked out over the little square in front of the church. The strangely silent crowd was beginning to fill it now, standing motionless beneath the heat that fell from the sky in nearly visible waves. Only the children ran around the square, stopping abruptly to light firecrackers that kept going off in quick succession. Seen from the balcony, the church, with its plaster walls, its dozen steps painted chalk blue, its two blue and gold towers, seemed smaller.

All at once the organ burst forth from inside the church. The crowd, gathered on the sides of the square, turned toward the portico. The men uncovered their heads, the women knelt down. For a long time the distant organ played a kind of slow march music. Then a strange sound of insect wings came from the forest. A tiny airplane with transparent wings and a frail fuselage, unexpected in this ageless world, emerged above the trees, swooped down above the square, and passed with a grinding rattle above the heads raised toward it. The plane then veered off toward the estuary.

But in the shadow of the church, an obscure bustling attracted attention again. The organ had fallen silent, overtaken now by brass and drums, invisible on the threshold. Penitents dressed in black surplices came out of the church one by one, gathered in groups on the portico, then began to go down the steps. Behind them came white penitents carrying red and blue banners, then a little troop of boys dressed like angels, societies of the Children of Mary, with their small, serious black faces. And at last, on a colorful reliquary borne by sweating dignitaries in their dark suits, stood an effigy of the good Lord Jesus himself, a reed in his hand, his head crowned with thorns, bleeding and tottering above the crowd that filled the steps of the portico.

When the reliquary reached the bottom of the steps, there was a pause while the penitents tried to arrange themselves in a semblance of order. It was then that d'Arrast saw the cook. He had just come out onto the portico, naked to the waist, carrying on his bearded head an enormous rectangular block resting on a cork mat on top of his skull. He came down the church steps with a firm tread, the stone precisely balanced in the arc of his short, muscular arms. When he stood behind the reliquary, the procession began to move. Then the musicians burst from the portico dressed in bright colored jackets and blowing into beribboned horns. To the rhythms of a quick march, the penitents stepped up their pace and reached one of the streets leading off the square. When the reliquary disappeared after them, nothing could be seen but the cook and the last musicians. Behind them, the crowd began to move amidst exploding firecrackers, while the airplane, with a great clash of pistons, circled back above the last of the procession. D'Arrast was looking only at the cook disappearing down the street; his shoulders, the engineer thought, were sagging. But at this distance he could not get a good look.

Through the empty streets, between closed stores and

locked doors, the judge, the chief of police, and d'Arrast reached the town hall. As they moved farther away from the fanfare and the exploding firecrackers, silence once more claimed the town, and already a few urubus were returning to the roofs where it seemed they had always lived. The town hall looked out onto a long, narrow street leading from one of the outlying quarters to the church square. For the moment it was empty. From the balcony of the town hall they could make out nothing but a pavement full of potholes where the recent rain had left several puddles. The sun, now slightly lower, was still devouring the blind facades of the houses on the other side of the street.

They waited a long time, so long that d'Arrast, watching the reflection of the sun on the wall across the street, once more felt the onset of fatigue and dizziness. The empty street, the abandoned houses, both attracted and sickened him. Again, he wanted to flee this country, and at the same time he was thinking about that enormous stone; he would have liked this trial to be over. He was about to propose going down to check the news when the church bells began to peal at full force. Just then, at the other end of the street to their left, a clamor burst forth and a crowd in a fever of excitement appeared. From a distance, clustered around the reliquary, pilgrims and penitents mingled and were advancing amidst firecrackers and shouts of joy along the narrow street. In a few seconds they filled it to overflowing, coming toward the town hall in an indescribable disorder—ages, races, and costumes melted into a motley mass covered with eyes and shouting mouths, an army of tapers issuing from it like lances with flames fading in the intense light. But when the crowd drew near, so dense beneath the balcony that it seemed to climb along the walls, d'Arrast saw that the cook was not there.

Without stopping to excuse himself, he left the balcony and the room, hurtled down the staircase and into the street beneath the thunder of bells and firecrackers. There he had to struggle against the joyful crowd, the taper bearers, and offended penitents. But insistently pushing with all his weight against the human tide, he cut a path with such abandon that he staggered and nearly fell when he found himself free, beyond the crowd, at the end of the street. Leaning against the burning wall, he waited to catch his breath. Then he continued on his way. At that moment, a group of men came into the street. The first were walking backward, and d'Arrast saw that they were surrounding the cook.

The man was visibly exhausted. He would stop, then, bent under the enormous stone, he would run a little, with the hurrying step of laborers and coolies, the rapid little trot of the wretched, the foot slapping the ground with its full weight. Around him, the penitents in surplices dirty with melted wax and dust encouraged him whenever he stopped. On his left, his brother was walking or running in silence. It seemed to d'Arrast that they were taking an interminable time to cover the space that separated them from him. Almost reaching him, the cook stopped again and looked around dully. When he saw d'Arrast—without seeming to recognize him—he stood still, turned toward him. An oily, dirty sweat covered his gray face; his beard was laced with saliva, a dry brown froth glued his lips. He tried to smile. But motionless beneath his burden, his whole body was trembling except for his shoulders, where the muscles were visibly knotted in a sort of cramp. The brother, who had recognized d'Arrast, said to him only: "He has fallen already." And Socrates, appearing out of nowhere, had just murmured in his ear: "Too much dancing, Monsieur d'Arrast, all night. He's tired."

The cook advanced again with his jerky trot, not like someone who wants to progress but as if he were fleeing a crushing burden, as if he were hoping to lighten it by moving. Without knowing how, d'Arrast found himself on his right. He put a hand lightly on the cook's back and walked beside him, with quick, heavy steps. At the other end of the street the reliquary had disappeared, and the crowd, which surely now filled the square, seemed to pause. For a few seconds, the cook, flanked by his brother and d'Arrast, gained some ground. Soon, barely twenty meters separated him from the group that had gathered before the town hall to watch him pass. Again, however, he stopped. D'Arrast's hand grew heavier. "Go on, cook," he said, "a little more." The other man was trembling; the saliva began to drip from his mouth again, while his whole body was literally spurting sweat. He took a deep breath and stopped short. He began to move again, took three steps, swayed. And suddenly the stone slipped onto his shoulder, gashing it, then down in front of him onto the ground, while the cook, losing his balance, collapsed on his side. Those in front of him leaped back, shouting encouragement; one of them grabbed the cork mat while others tried to lift the stone onto him again.

Leaning over him, d'Arrast used a hand to clean the blood and dust from the smaller man's shoulder as he lay facedown on the earth, gasping for breath. He heard nothing and did not move. His mouth opened avidly with each breath, as if it were his last. D'Arrast clasped him under the arms and lifted him as easily as if he were a child, holding him tightly against himself. Leaning with all his height, he spoke into the cook's face, as if to imbue him with his own strength. After a moment, the other man, bleeding and dirty, detached himself with a haggard expression. He staggered once more toward the stone, which the others were raising a little. But he stopped, looking at the stone with a vacant stare, and shook his head. Then he let his arms fall to his sides and turned toward d'Arrast. Huge tears ran silently down his ravaged face. He wanted to speak, he was speaking, but his mouth hardly formed the syllables. "I promised," he was saying. And then: "Ah, Captain! Ah, Captain!" and the tears drowned his voice. His brother came up behind him, took him in his arms, and the cook, weeping, let himself go slack against him, defeated, his head lolling back.

D'Arrast looked at him but could find no words. He turned toward the crowd in the distance, now shouting again. Suddenly, he snatched the cork mat from the hands holding it and walked toward the stone. He gestured to the others to lift it and took it almost effortlessly. Slightly compressed beneath the weight of the stone, his shoulders hunched, panting a little, he looked down at his feet, listening to the cook's sobs. Then he began moving on his own with a vigorous stride, steadily crossing the space that separated him from the crowd at the end of the street, and cut a path decisively through the first rows, which stood aside to let him pass. He entered the square between two rows of spectators, suddenly gone silent and looking at him in astonishment amidst the din of church bells and exploding firecrackers. He was advancing with the same resolute step, and the crowd opened a path for him up to the church. Despite the weight that was beginning to crush his head and neck, he saw the church and the reliquary, which seemed to be waiting for him on the portico. He was walking toward it and had already passed the center of the square when abruptly, without knowing why, he veered to the left and turned away from the path to the church, forcing the pilgrims to face him. Behind him, he could hear someone running. In front of him, everyone was openmouthed. He did not understand what they were shouting, although he seemed to recognize the Portuguese word they kept hurling at him. Suddenly, Socrates appeared in front of him, rolling his frightened eyes, speaking incoherently and pointing out the path to the church behind him. "To the church, to the church"—that was what Socrates and the crowd were shouting to him. D'Arrast, however, continued on his way. And Socrates stepped aside, his arms comically raised to the sky, while the crowd gradually quieted down. When d'Arrast entered the first street, familiar to him from his stroll to the riverside quarters with

the cook, the square was no more than a vague murmur behind him.

The stone now weighed painfully on his head and he
needed all the strength of his huge arms to lighten it. By the
time he reached the first streets with their slippery incline, his
shoulders were already knotted. He stopped to listen. He was
alone. He straightened the stone on its cork support and went
down cautiously but steadily toward the huts. When he got
there, he was nearly out of breath, and his arms were trembling around the stone. He walked faster, finally reached the
little square where the cook's hut stood, ran to it, kicked open
the door, and in one movement heaved the stone into the
center of the room, onto the still-glowing fire. And there,
straightening up to his full height, suddenly enormous, inhal-
ing with desperate gulps the familiar smell of poverty and
ashes, he listened to the wave of joy surging inside him, dark
and panting, which he could not name.

When the hut's inhabitants arrived, they found d'Arrast
standing against the back wall, his eyes closed. In the center of
the room, in the hearth space, the stone was half-buried in
cinders and earth. They stood on the threshold without coming in and stared at d'Arrast in silence, as if questioning him.
But he was quiet. Then the brother led the cook to the stone,
where he let himself drop to the ground. The brother sat
down too, gesturing to the others. The old woman joined
him, then the young girl of the night before, but no one was
looking at d'Arrast. They were squatting silently around the

stone. Only the murmur of the river rose to them through the heavy air. Standing in the dark, d'Arrast was listening without seeing anything, and the sound of the waters filled him with a tumultuous happiness. His eyes closed, he joyously honored his own strength, honored once more the life that was beginning again. At the same moment, a firecracker exploded nearby. The brother moved away a little from the cook and, half turning toward d'Arrast, without looking at him, motioned him to an empty place: "Sit down with us."

ALSO BY ALBERT CAMUS

THE FIRST MAN

Published thirty-five years after its discovery, *The First Man* tells the story of Jacques Cormery, a boy who lived a life much like Camus's own—a childhood circumscribed by poverty and a father's death, yet redeemed by the austere beauty of Algeria and the boy's attachment to his nearly deaf-mute mother.

Fiction/Literature/978-0-679-76816-6

THE PLAGUE

In Oran, a coastal town in North Africa, the plague begins as a series of portents and gradually becomes an omnipresent reality, obliterating all traces of the past and driving its victims to almost unearthly extremes of suffering, madness, and compassion.

Fiction/Literature/978-0-679-72021-8

THE STRANGER

Through this story of an ordinary man who unwittingly gets drawn into a senseless murder on a sun-drenched Algerian beach, Camus explored what he termed "the nakedness of man faced with the absurd."

Fiction/Literature/978-0-679-72020-1

ALSO AVAILABLE:

Caligula and Three Other Plays, 978-0-394-70207-0
The Fall, 978-0-679-72022-5
A Happy Death, 978-0-679-76400-7
Lyrical and Critical Essays, 978-0-394-70852-2
The Myth of Sisyphus, 978-0-679-73373-7
The Rebel: An Essay on Man in Revolt, 978-0-679-73384-3
Resistance, Rebellion, and Death, 978-0-679-76401-4

VINTAGE BOOKS
Available at your local bookstore, or call toll-free to order:
1-800-793-2665 (credit cards only).